# QUATERMAIN

## THE NEW ADVENTURES

AIRSHIP 27 PRODUCTIONS

Quatermain:The New Adventures

Published by Airship 27 Productions
www.airship27.com
www.airship27hangar.com

Editor: Ron Fortier
Associate Editor: Charles Saunders
Production and design by Rob Davis.

ISBN-13: 978-0615834986
ISBN-10:0615834981

Printed in the United States of America

10 9 8 7 6 5 4 3 2 1

# QUATERMAIN
## THE NEW ADVENTURES
## TABLE OF CONTENTS

# GOLDEN IVORY

## BY ALAN J. PORTER

In all the years I've listened to family tales of days and generations past the vast majority of the stories have been of my mother's ancestors; and why not? For her antecedents include royal regents, castle jailers, and lady pirates. Of my father's family I heard little, with the single exception of my great Uncle Norman. Although I only knew him in his declining years his youth was one of adventure and action. He was one of the first dirt track motorcycle racers in the country, and during the First World War served not in the trenches of France, but in the oft overlooked theater of North Africa.

This later fact provides the catalyst for the narrative that follows, for recently I was sent a box of old Uncle Norman's papers, amongst which were numerous leaves of unbound paper recounting a story he had been told during his years of military service. Written on the top most sheet, in his distinctive hand, was the following:

*The tale that follows is true. Or at least I believe it to be so, for I have no reason to doubt the word of the gentleman who took great pains to tell me his story in the fullest detail. The recounting of this tale took several evenings of concentrated effort on the part of the storyteller, an effort to which he invested considerable effort and strength; for the raconteur was a man of advancing years.*

*I first encountered the storyteller in the lobby of a hotel in Alexandria where I had recently arrived with a dispatch for some General or other. My interest in, and skills on, motorcycles had resulted in me being allocated the role of dispatch rider for the Manchester Regiment. A role I was happy to take on, for although there were dangers attached, the joy of riding bikes at speed over difficult terrain, and the occasional night in a good soft bed, when delivering messages to headquarters staff, often compensated for the less savory aspects of the task.*

*This was such an occasion, and whilst waiting for my billet I was accosted by this well spoken gentleman of advanced age who informed me that I reminded him of a former companion, also a British soldier, and requested that in exchange for a drink that I should listen as he recounted the story of his erstwhile colleague and friend. With nothing better to do while I waited, and the offer of a free drink fresh in my mind, I agreed. This is his tale.*

Elephants! Always elephants. That's all he ever wanted to talk about. The man was a legend along the riverbanks and beyond. Everywhere I took my boat I heard tales. He called himself an elephant hunter, but if the stories I'd heard were even a fraction of the truth, he was so much more.

I mean it's true that jungle tales of men's deeds have a habit of growing at a prodigious speed with each retelling, and by the time the story takes residence in your typical riverside bar its resemblance to anything close to the facts that started the process is little more than cursory at best. Yet when you start to hear the same name being repeated, and when the basic aspects of the exploits being recounted contain the same incidents and general outcomes, then you have to begin to believe that there is more than a grain of truth hidden among the hyperbole.

The tales I'd heard had convinced me that I was in search of the right man to help me solve the mystery that had been dropped in my lap.

Well to be strictly accurate it had actually been dropped in my hat.

Over my years as a riverboat trader, for that was my profession at the time, I had received many strange items in lieu of payment, some of which had an uncertain provenance but undoubtedly had links to the jungle's interior. It wasn't unknown for some tribes to coat trinkets in various obnoxious, and occasionally fatal, substances that could lay a man low through the tiniest of scratches. After one or two close calls with such substances I developed the habit of insisting that when anyone offered objects in trade, that they should drop them into my hat rather than my hands. At first the practice offended a few of my business associates, but over time it became accepted as just one of my quirks, of which I will readily admit I have several. Anyway I'm convinced it has saved me from further discomfort, and possibly death, on a few occasions since.

The hat full of trinkets that provided the catalyst for this adventure came from a particularly undistinguished specimen of humanity that I had the unfortunate distinction of having to do business with on a semi-regular basis. He told me his name was Karl, and he appeared to be of Germanic descent, other than that I knew nothing of him, and nor do I wish to find out more.

Nor do I recall what exactly the trade was for, but given Karl's normal habits it was more than likely to be a less than healthy combination of liquor, firearms, and saucy postcards from Paris. The man had strange tastes, but I'm no missionary, and it wasn't my place to question his morals. As long as he paid in either cash or trade I was fine with letting him live his debauched life any way he chose.

On this particular occasion he had cash. A lot of it; and seemed to be overly pleased with himself. In fact, instead of his usual curt, brash, Germanic self he was almost approaching being loquacious. Inviting me to stay and enjoy sharing a bottle of schnapps that I had just transported up river for him. I guess this is why that particular transaction stayed in my mind, beyond it being the catalyst for subsequent events that is. He had never shown the slightest inclination towards being sociable; never mind sharing a drink with me. The drink, as it tends to, loosened his tongue to an extent that I had never experienced before. Thankfully he spared me his life story and instead started to spin some yarn about how he had stumbled upon a scheme that would make him rich enough that he would soon be able to leave the steamy jungles of the Dark Continent behind. As I'd never expressed any interest in what had bought him to Africa in the first instance, nor why he stayed, I had little interest in anything that would speed his departure. It would have no impact on my life, or so I thought, so did not really listen to his almost incoherent ramblings. How wrong I was on that assumption, and now wished I had in fact focused on my erstwhile companion's sodden ramblings as they may have eased future burdens. But I am getting ahead of myself in my narrative.

As we finished our liquid repast Karl dropped a handful of trinkets into my hat as a farewell gesture, unnecessary, as he had already paid in full, an equally uncharacteristic gesture as had been the rest of his behavior that day.

I must admit that after my return downstream to the coast to replenish my supplies and secure further cargo I gave little thought to the German or his parting gift, which by now had been unceremoniously deposited at the back of a small foot locker in the stern of the *Lucky Lucy*, for that was the name of my riverboat. There it stayed for several months until the day that I happened to be floating past the area of riverbank where Karl had kept camp. Even though I had no deliveries for him I pulled ashore, more out of mild curiosity than any concern for his well-being. Sure enough it seemed that his wild story might have held some truth, for his camp was abandoned, and looked like it had been so for some time. I guess his talk of a grand scheme had been legitimate and that he had managed to buy his way out of Africa. I will admit that the thought of Karl's possible financial windfall made me curious about his half-forgotten parting gift to me.

When he had dropped the trinkets into my hat at our parting those months before they had been in a small drawstring bag, and there they had remained. Now, as I sat on the side of the *Lucky Lucy*, I pulled at those same drawstrings with a mix of skepticism and curiosity, wondering what bequest this strange man had left in my possession. Once the bag was open I poured the contents out on to an old oily rag I kept hanging close to the boat's engine.

At first glance the motley collection of objects seemed unremarkable; a small compass which, judging by the series of scratches around the periphery of the dial, had seen better days, a primitive arrow head from some native weapon, although the design was unfamiliar to me, the end of a tusk, and one of those singular Parisian post cards.

I must have sat staring at this strange collection of objects for well over an hour as I tried to decipher their meaning, for the shadows grew longer as the sun descended towards the end of the day. As the setting orb reached a particular height just below the tree tops a shaft of light struck the remnant of tusk at an angle. It glittered.

This caught my attention, as I hadn't noticed it being inlayed or festooned with any adornments on my first cursory glance. Picking the tusk up for a closer look it sparkled in the shaft of sunlight, yet, as I had earlier surmised, it was without decoration or gilding. I must admit to being puzzled as I turned the tusk over and over in my hand. Then the realization came to me. The tusk glittered with a pure golden sheen. It wasn't overlaid with gold, nor had gold been inserted into its surface by skilled artisans, nor was it a golden model of a tusk. It felt and looked like the ivory tusk of a typical elephant, yet woven into the structure, organically, as if a natural part of the structure were what appeared to be flecks of gold. For want of a better term what I held in my hand was golden ivory.

I know, I can almost hear you saying it to yourself, "the man's insane, there's no such thing as golden ivory." I will admit that I doubted my sanity at first, but it was difficult to deny the evidence of my own eyes. I decided I needed a second opinion.

However I did not want to go about broadcasting the news of my strange discovery abroad. Some sort of premonition seemed to dictate that I should be wary of who I trusted.

So not to arouse any suspicion regarding potential changes to my routine, after leaving Karl's deserted campsite I continued up river to complete my scheduled deliveries. In fact I kept to my regular schedule for the next three months, during which time I formulated a plan on how I could possibly track down someone who could assist me.

But, as has been proven to me many times in my life, the most thought through and detailed planning is no match for serendipity.

Truth be told I had just about given up any hope of arriving at a suitable course of action that would allow me to peruse the mystery of the strange tusk. But while contemplating my failure over a tankard of something that passed for ale in a dark coastal bar, fate decided to step in. While I stared at the liquid in my cup my mind had started to wander, not really focused on anything in particular. Snatches of conversation from various patrons began to creep into the edges of my subconscious. Slowly the conversation of two men in particular began to rise over the general drone of voices. It was not so much the topic of conversation, as I couldn't really make that out, but the tone and cadence. Decidedly English, something that as a Canadian I am sometimes mistaken for to those with an uneducated ear for the finer subtleties of the Empire's accents.

Then one uttered a word, and I knew that I had to interject and introduce myself; for it was a word I'd been waiting to hear these last months. In fact it wasn't so much a word as a name. A surname.

"Quatermain."

There it was again, the very name I've been searching for, but the second time I heard it the tone behind it displayed an underpinning of annoyance. As I approached I also realized that this second mention of the name came from a new direction and was in an accent that definitely wasn't English.

As this new fact registered I was suddenly spun around as a large heavyset mass of muscle collided with my right shoulder and arm. As well as unbalancing me, the force of the collision resulted in an even more dire consequence, the loss of the watery beer I had been carrying. It's true that the liquid refreshment offered in this African coastal drinking establishment bore only a passing resemblance to the beverages served in more civilized parts of the world. In fact it resembled beer in name only. But it was the only thing available, and after several weeks on the river, at this moment it was as precious to me as the finest champagne would be to a socialite in a Paris salon.

After I completed my involuntary rotation, I reached out with my now empty right hand and tapped the broad shoulders of the culprit who caused my sudden alcoholic bereavement.

My touch had no impact. The behemoth continued on his path towards the two Englishmen at the bar. As we seemed to share a common destination, I followed.

Another couple of attempts to try and attract his attention also failed to elicit any response, and on each instance my frustration grew in step. I momentarily forgot about the focus of my initial search, and attracting this man's attention became all-consuming. He came to a sudden halt a few feet short of the bar. In my current state my reactions were somewhat compromised from their natural effectiveness, and I failed to follow his example. I plowed straight into him, at considerable speed.

You know the common idiom of "be careful what you wish for"? Well it certainly applied in this case. I had been hoping to catch this man's attention, and now I had achieved that goal.

The larger bulk in front of me, which I estimated to be at least twenty stone in weight on a six-foot plus frame, turned slowly and stared at me.

"What is your problem?" The voice was deep. Each word enunciated slowly as if English wasn't his natural tongue, a supposition supported by the underlying French accent.

"You owe me a drink."

"Why would you say that? I have never seen you before, little man." If the "little man" comment was meant as an insult, it didn't really work as everyone in the bar could be viewed as being of a diminutive stature when compared to the speaker.

"You knocked the drink out of my hand as you pushed your way to the bar." I explained.

The face in front of me remained impassive. "So?"

"So you owe me a drink." I repeated.

"Go away. I have business to discuss." With that he dismissed me as being inconsequential. Not a position I relish, nor appreciate. I will admit that at this point, although I like to think of myself as a level headed man, my temper got the better of me. Knowing that I could never match this man for size and bulk, I decided to invoke surprise. I turned as if to indicate that his dismissive command had been effective. Having taken half a step away and then suddenly tensed, spun round, and launched myself at his back with all my pent up rage.

So much for the element of surprise.

I'm still not sure how he became aware of my movement, maybe he heard me, or caught my sudden movement out of the corner of his eye. Despite his mass he moved as quickly and fluidly as a man half his size.

If truth be told he didn't actually move in terms of taking a step, he just leaned over to his right. As a result my charge carried me past his left hand side. My feet caught and tripped over his planted left foot launching me even further forward into the man that stood at the bar. The man who had been the object of his shouted greeting a few moments before.

And that is how I first made the acquaintance of Allan Quatermain, by falling head long into his stomach.

I would have expected a man of Quatermain's apparent age to collapse on such an impact, but for all the effect I had on him I may have been just another of the interminable tsetse flies that are an ever present nuisance in that part of the continent. He literally brushed me off as easily as he would the previously mentioned insect. His bar companion was another matter entirely.

"How dare you?" His cry expressed pure outrage, and with that he reached down a calloused hand, and grabbed the collar of my shirt, by which he dragged me to my feet. A fact that impressed me as much for the fact that the frayed collar stayed attached to my old torn shirt, as for the strength it displayed.

Once on my feet I stood eye to eye with the new player in this growing complex scenario.

"You, sir, need to apologize." The delivery was more of an order than a request.

"It wasn't my fault…" I started, somewhat hesitantly not sure how he would react to what, even to my own ears, sounded like a poor excuse. He looked at me with a smirk on his face.

"That wasn't directed at you, river rat. It was meant for the brute whose action caused your unintended flight into my companion here."

I shifted my gaze to look in the direction of the object of his command.

"Moi?" The deep voice rumbled in response. "Are you talking to moi?"

"Yes I was, sir," repeated the challenger. "And despite your dubious French manners, you still need to apologize."

"Honestly, Sergeant Cunningham, there is no need for that. In fact from this brute's demeanor I would think that delivering an apology was not part of his agenda in locating me."

"With all due respect, Mr. Quatermain, sir. No matter his original intent, I believe he still needs to apologize."

"You should listen to the old man, mon ami. I was paid to find him and teach him a lesson, but I will be happy to include you for free."

"You can try." The man I now knew to be called Cunningham, roared back, as he stepped closer to the Frenchman. As he did so Quatermain tried to put a restraining arm on his military companion's arm. With each passing second the situation was getting tenser. As the three men squared up to each other, I slipped away deciding that discretion was perhaps the better part of valor after all. The tension in the bar was palpable, and my hard won experience of being in several similar situations over the years had taught me we had reached the tipping point. In the next few seconds the situation would calm down and the various parties would step back; or some stupid move would serve as the spark that would result in a full blown bar brawl.

Someone created the spark.

On reflection I'm still not sure what started it. It may have been a thrown bottle or tankard, although more likely a punch thrown over some imagined transgression by a disgruntled customer. Whatever it was, the bar suddenly erupted in a display of violence and cursing. Bottles and fists flew along with various verbal invectives. A hurricane of violence, and in the middle of it, the eye at the center of the storm remained the three figures of Quatermain, the soldier, and the Frenchman. Cunningham was poised as if trying to stand protection for the older man, but it was a futile gesture. As I previously noted, the melee seemed to swirl around them. It was as if, even in the midst of a full throw down punch up, that the figure of Allan Quatermain remained somehow sacrosanct to the denizens of the bar. He was not to be touched.

The one person who had clearly made his ignorance of this local tradition apparent was, of course, the brutish Frenchman; who it appeared had been sent to deliver a warning to Quatermain to avoid becoming involved in someone's business (whose business that was I never found out). Once again the Frenchman lurched in the direction of his target. Quatermain simply stood his ground and, as his opponent descended on him, threw a perfectly timed round house punch that caught the larger man squarely on his jaw, instantly dropping him to the floor like a sack of last week's potatoes.

Cunningham straightened up from his defensive posture and looked with admiration at Quatermain, for it was now perfectly clear that the older man needed no protection. "I say Mr. Quatermain, sir, that was a resoundingly successful punch."

Quatermain simply smiled and bowed slightly in the direction of his now recumbent opponent, "Thank you, but I suggest that we continue our discussion elsewhere before he wakes up."

The two men stepped over the Frenchman and headed for the establishment's outer doors, the heaving mass of brawling humanity parting before them like the waves of the Red Sea.

I hastily followed.

'Mr. Quatermain!" I shouted after them as we reached the street outside, "May I have a word?"

The two stopped and looked back in my direction. Cunningham visibly stiffened when he recognized me. He scoffed "It's only the river rat."

Quatermain ignored the jibe and beckoned me forward to join them. "And what can I do for you Monsieur Negreau?"

I must admit to being somewhat taken aback that he knew my name. "Call me Daniel, please. I'm not one for formality."

"So I've heard." The soldier snarled again, a habit I was quietly coming to dislike. At some point I knew I would have to teach this prig a thing or two about how to deal with people in Africa. His Imperial British superior airs and graces when dealing with colonials and other foreigners wouldn't get him very far in this country.

Quatermain, again ignoring Cunningham's remark, held out his hand in greeting, "Daniel, it is then. And I would still like to know what it is that I can do for you?"

"I have some ivory I need you to look at."

"I think I've seen enough ivory to last me a lifetime, and to be honest I'm not really interested in seeing any more."

I reached for the bag at my side, "I would be surprised if you've seen any like this before."

Quatermain reached out and placed his sun-leathered and calloused hand over mine stopping me from opening the bag. "I wouldn't go showing off the fact that you're carrying valuables around here. Come to the UE offices in about an hour and we can talk. First I have another rendezvous to keep."

"An hour then." I agreed.

"Splendid." And with that Quatermain and Cunningham stepped away and melted into the milling dockside crowds.

At the appointed time I found myself in front of the offices of Union & Empire Exports Ltd. Although they were ostensibly in the import/ export business I had never conducted business with UE, as they were colloquially known, nor had any other river or jungle trader that I knew. What exactly UE imported and, or, exported was something of a mystery. It was rumored that they had some sort of special government contract

*"...what it is that I can do for you?"*

and were well connected back in London, but nothing of substance ever came to light to back-up that supposition.

I was about to knock on the outer door when Cunningham opened it from the inside. I had a suspicion he had been watching, waiting for my arrival. He invited me in, his tone a little friendlier than it had been an hour previously. Stepping inside I took a quick look around the room. I must admit that after all the mystery and rumor surrounding this place that I was disappointed to see that it looked just like the business office of any other trading company. But with perhaps one exception, for it gradually dawned on me that everything was just a little too neat and organized, as if on display rather being where it was as a result of everyday use.

Before I could assimilate this observation any further a now familiar voice greeted me.

"Good afternoon, Daniel. Glad you could make it." Quatermain was sat at a table over to one side of the room. Several maps were spread out on the table in front of him. Sitting alongside him was a small rotund man who, from the tone of his skin, and the manner of his dress, obviously hailed from the Indian sub-continent. Following my gaze Quatermain gestured in the direction of his guest. "Let me introduce you. This is Rajesh. He is something of an expert on elephants, and as that is the topic you said you wanted to discus I thought it would be pertinent if he joined us. So what do you want to show us?" 'Us' not 'me.' Quatermain had let me know that whatever I wanted to share I was going to have to do it with everyone in the room.

I must admit that I wasn't enamored with the idea of telling too many people about Karl's gift, but if Quatermain trusted Cunningham and this Indian Rajesh, then I guess I felt I should too. I unclipped the bag from my belt and walked across the room towards the table, noticing that as soon as I moved in their direction the Rajesh fellow immediately rolled up the maps and pushed them to one side. I also heard Cunningham behind me click the office door shut, which closed off a lot of natural light throwing the majority of the room into gloom. What shafts of afternoon sunlight that remained came through the window shutters and illuminated the tabletop.

Reaching the table I opened the drawstring at the top of the bag and poured its odd contents out for all to see.

"A strange pot-pourri of items to be sure," Rajesh spoke for the first time, his voice more educated than I'd first suspected. Definite traces of English public school tones underlying his native tongue.

Picking up the ivory I passed it to Quatermain. "This is the piece I need your advice on."

Quatermain slowly rotated it between thumb and forefinger. "A nice piece for sure, Daniel, but what is it you need to know about it?"

"Put it in the shaft of sunlight, then slowly rotate it." I instructed.

Quatermain did as I directed. This time as he turned the piece everyone in the room could see the golden interwoven effect I previously described. I heard a low appreciative whistle come from Cunningham who was still stood behind me.

"Golden ivory?" I said.

"At first glance it would appear to be something like that, yes," confirmed Quatermain. "What do you think, Rajesh?"

We all glanced across at the Indian, expecting him to pass a verdict on the golden sight in front of him. Instead of looking at the ivory he had picked up, and was staring at, the somewhat salacious Parisian postcard that Karl had included in his going away package. When he realized that we were all looking at him, the Indian gave an embarrassed cough and dropped the card back on the table with a muttered "Remarkable." Then he pointed at the glinting ivory between Quatermain's fingers, "Yes, quite remarkable. Where did you get it?"

I then proceeded to recount the story of my last encounter with Karl, his pronouncement, and his bizarre parting gifts. Cunningham in particular seemed very interested in Karl and his background, asking a lot of questions which frankly I did not have the answers for.

After I completed my narrative the three men sat in silence looking at each other, as if in silent communication.

The silence was eventually broken by Rajesh. "Mr. Negreau, your timing is fortuitous. As you may have surmised, just before your arrival in this office Messrs Quatermain, Cunningham, and I were planning a trip." With that he nodded in the direction of the rolled up maps at the end of the table. "Based on our previous conversations we would be in need of a river boat for the first leg of our journey. Would you be interested in providing that service?"

"What about the ivory?" I asked, "I really came here to find out if it was for real, not sign on for another trip."

"Oh it's quite real," intoned Rajesh, "and if you would care to join us on the rest of our journey I believe you will find the answer to all your questions regarding the provenance and authenticity of the 'golden ivory' as you have christened it."

"I can take you up river for sure, but a full expedition into the interior? I'm not sure I can be away from my regular routes for that long. I have a living to make."

"We could use a man of your skills and fortitude, Daniel," Quatermain added, almost pleading with me.

"I have been fully authorized to cover whatever costs our excursion needs," added Rajesh. "I can arrange a substantial payment through these very offices to cover both your craft rental and your time for an extended absence from your river trade." He smiled, almost conspiratorially. "In much the same way that I have engaged the services of Messrs Quatermain and Cunningham for their particular areas of expertise."

Well that surprised me. The Indian was the boss of whatever jaunt it was they were putting together. I'd assumed it was Quatermain. I guess despite the legends he was, at the end of the day, someone who needed to cover his costs just like anyone else. Elephant hunter for hire, just like I was a boatman for hire; at least that's what I thought of myself as. Little did I realize that the exchange I'd had in that strange dusty office would change my fate so drastically in the weeks ahead.

Hippopotamuses. Do you realize how much of a risk to riverboats those things are? Nobody thinks they are dangerous. Crocodiles, sure, river snakes, sure, but not hippos. They are just dumb slow moving river horses. But you'd be surprised. Cunningham wouldn't believe me either, until the day I pulled him from the river.

The start of the river journey had been uneventful, as had the ten days since. Well except for the usual frictions of four head-strong men forced together in the confines of a small riverboat.

Quatermain seemed the best suited to such conditions, keeping to himself, and rarely talking much. When we could persuade him into discourse he mainly spoke, with a clear send of paternal pride, about his son in London. The thing he wouldn't really talk about was the very things the rest of us wanted to hear; tales of his legendary exploits as a hunter and guide. It seemed that the real life Allan Quatermain had little interest in the Allan Quatermain of jungle gossip and bar side chatter.

The Indian, Rajesh, was quite the opposite. He seemed to enjoy the sound of his own voice, sometimes to an irritating degree. He could prattle on about the most inconsequential things. However as the days passed I slowly began to realize that while he spoke a lot, he actually said very little. His prattle and questions also seemed to invoke both Cunningham and myself to perhaps reveal more of ourselves than we would normally be comfortable with.

Now Cunningham, there was a strange fish if ever I've met one. On first impression at the bar and in the office he struck me as nothing more than your typical career army man, just following orders. Although whose I couldn't figure out. But I couldn't have been more wrong. As it turned out we were alike, perhaps too alike in temperament, if not in personal habits.

I'll admit I was a slovenly character, not too bothered about personal hygiene, I mean why bother when most of the time you are on your own aboard a river boat plowing your way through a hot and humid jungle. It's not exactly the best environment to encourage maintaining a groomed look. My lack of cleanliness also extended to the upkeep of the *Lucky Lucy*. She may have looked a mess, but I knew where everything was. It was this difference in opinion that eventually led to the situation where Sergeant Cunningham needed to be extricated from the river.

"How can you live like this Negreau?" It was the morning of the twelfth day on the river, and the Sergeant was waving what appeared to be one of my two shirts in my direction. I must admit from the distance of twenty feet at the other end of the *Lucky Lucy*, I wasn't sure if it was actually one of my shirts. It could have been anyone of the multitude of oily rags that lay around various surfaces and crevices on my vessel. I was guessing it was a shirt as he stood close by the locker where I tended to throw my clothing.

"Live like what?" I called back, for I must admit I was genuinely puzzled by his question.

"In this floating pig sty?"

"Be careful Sergeant. I won't have anyone besmirch the name of my *Lucy*."

"I wasn't insulting your boat, River Rat, more you and your slovenly habits. This is no way for a business man to present himself." He started waving the cloth around a bit more vigorously. If he let go I had visions of it sailing over the side and into the river. "And what do you call this?" He continued twirling.

"My second best shirt, I think," I responded, "and stop waving it about like that, it'll end up in the river."

"Now there's an idea. It could certainly do with a wash. As could you and every other scrap of stinking cloth on this tub." And with that he let go, and as I'd predicted my shirt traversed a perfect arc into the water.

I may not take much care of the few clothes I own, but I certainly object to them being casually disposed of. I rushed to the back of the boat and headed for the side where my vestment had disappeared. As I reached the boat rail, I felt Cunningham's hand on my shoulder. "Let it go, it could do with the wash. As could you. On second thoughts perhaps you should join it." And with that I felt him start to push me forward over the side, laughing as he did so. He may have seen it as a joke, but I didn't. There were certain stretches of the river where the last place you wanted to be was in the water, and this was one of those.

I didn't have time to explain why I was opposed to an involuntary swim, so took the shortest action possible. I kicked backwards and caught Cunningham across the shin with the sole of my boot. The Sergeant's howl, a combination of pain, surprise, and rage, was enough to awaken Rajesh and Quatermain who had been slumbering nearby. Quatermain seemed to size up the situation in an instant and pointed Rajesh in the direction of the boat's wheel while he headed aft to try and break up our altercation.

"Why you bugger..." Cunningham screamed at me while hopping up and down on one leg while grasping his bleeding shin between clasped hands. To be honest it was a fairly comical sight, but that wasn't an observation the rest of the boat's occupants felt like sharing. Cunningham took a hop forward, released his hands and made a swing at me. "I ought to knock your block off for that."

"You were the one throwing my clothes overboard. I'm only trying to protect my possessions. I have few enough as it is without you disposing of them."

"Well maybe I should have thrown you in after them, seeing you're so fond of those tatty rags." And with that he took another lurch towards me. As he did so the *Lucky Lucy* suddenly shifted sideways in the water. It wasn't a shift in current. It was a sudden movement as if we'd hit something.

I looked back towards the bow and saw Rajesh apparently struggling with the wheel. "What's going on?" I shouted. Concern for my boat overriding any concern for my sodden clothes or the angry Army Sergeant bearing down on me.

"The rocks!" Rajesh was pointing excitedly off the port bow, "They are moving."

"What do you mean the rocks are mov..." Suddenly I knew what was happening. "HOLD ON!" I shouted. "Everyone hold on."

The boat rose upwards as it was bodily lifted out of the water. I looked back to check on my passengers just in time to witness Quatermain let go of his hand hold and dive forward. "NO!" I called out. Quatermain hit the deck and grabbed on to a rope tie-ring with his left hand, while his right arm stretched out in front of him just short of what he had been trying to catch, a toppling Sergeant Cunningham. As the boat continued to rock I could only watch helpless as the Army man toppled over the side and into the now churning waters around us.

There was nothing we could do until the boat settled; otherwise we would be joining him.

"What's happening?" called Rajesh, still struggling to get some sort of control on the spinning tiller wheel and bucking craft.

"Hippos!" I shouted back. "We must have drifted into their territory. This could get really bad, really quickly."

Just as quickly as we'd been thrust upwards, the boat suddenly settled back down. I reckoned we had maybe ten or fifteen seconds before the next hit. Hippos rarely attack a boat at mid-point, they prefer to capsize the craft and then make short work of the occupants. They may look like docile "water-horses" but when they feel threatened they are vicious and the large canine teeth make them one of the most feared killers in the African jungle.

Cunningham's thrashing about in the water was almost as good as a painted sign saying, "Eat Me."

I reckoned that the hippo underneath us would try and reposition itself under the prow to have another go at capsizing us. "Try to hold her steady, if you can." I called to Rajesh.

With my orders issued (I did occasionally actually act as the vessel's Captain), my next focus was getting Cunningham out of the water as soon as possible. It wouldn't take long for his thrashing to attract another irritated hippo, if it hadn't already done so. As I switched my attention back towards the stern I was amazed to see that Quatermain was ahead of me in my thinking. He was stood with one foot firmly planted on the side rail to give him purchase, with a rope circled around his waist and anchored to the ring he had been gripping mere moments before. The free end of the rope was already over the side, where Quatermain had thrown it. The rope had an empty tin can attached to its free end to act as a floatation device so it wouldn't sink, and was easy for the man in the water to see and grab hold off.

There was little else for me to do other than take up position alongside Quatermain and add my strength to the rope. "Impressive" I muttered at the elephant hunter as I took up my position. He did little but grunt in acknowledgment, his focus being entirely on the task at hand.

"Sergeant Cunningham, stay still. Just float if you can." Quatermain shouted. A good plan in theory, as movement would attract an attacking animal. But theory is often overwritten by the reality of being in the water pursued by two-tons of angry bull hippo. I will give the Sergeant his due, in that he calmed down a little.

"Grab the can and we'll haul you in." I shouted.

Cunningham lunged for the can, and missed. His momentum carried him under the surface and he disappeared from view. As we searched for any sign of the man under the water Quatermain and I spotted the large grey shape of the male hippo that was coming back around for another attack on the boat. Of Cunningham there was no sign.

Suddenly I heard a splash next to me, and just caught the sight of Quatermain's legs as he too disappeared under the water. "What the hell?" I called to no one in particular, and as I was now on my own at that end of the boat no-one was around to hear me anyway. "Is he trying to get himself killed too?"

As I finished my rhetorical thought Quatermain broke surface, and I could see that he was holding on to an unconscious Cunningham. Quatermain kicked out to drive himself and his burden back in the direction of the *Lucky Lucy*. The large grey shape followed. Just as Quatermain reached the side of the boat the jaws of the massive bull hippo broke the water; its mouth open displaying the gigantic canine teeth.

The jaws closed. Right on Cunningham's floating leg, for the unconscious man was in no state to react and pull his limbs in closer to the boat. I watch, amazed, as Quatermain let go of the side of the boat and lunged in he creature's direction. As he thrust outwards he shouted, "When I make contact, pull Cunningham free and on board."

I leant over and grabbed the collar of Cunningham's uniform hoping that it would hold. As I did so Quatermain struck the hippo in the eye with his fist. It roared in rage and as the giant mouth opened I pulled Cunningham free and over the rail back into the boat. His sodden mass landed on top of me driving me to the floor leaving me unsighted on Quatermain's fate. I was convinced that he had sealed his own fate whilst rescuing our military companion.

A tap on my shoulder proved me wrong, as there stood over me was a wet, but very much alive, elephant hunter.

"How...?" I looked at him quizzically.

"As soon as I hit it I let the arc of my lunge carry me under and swam back under the boat, climbing up the other side. But we aren't out of it yet."

I rolled the recumbent Cunningham off me, and as I did so I noticed that I was covered in his blood. A large gash had been opened on his leg, undoubtedly where he had been dragged against the hippo's large tooth. "I'll dress that," shouted Quatermain, "you get us out of here."

I bounded forward, and without a word took control of the wheel from Rajesh, who didn't object to my taking command. I steered the boat as far as I could to starboard to get us back on the other side of the river and out of the hippo's territory. Why they didn't pursue the attack, I'm not sure, but whatever the reason, the bull seemed to think his point had been made and left us alone. It had all happened in the space of perhaps a few seconds, but now we could relax again and tend to our comrade's wounds.

So I thought. Right up to the moment when I remembered which stretch of the river we were on. Now I knew why the hippo hadn't chased us. There was a reason its territory didn't cover this stretch of water. The rapids.

Having survived one attack, the *Lucky Lucy* was about to undergo another, and I just prayed that that she would live up to her name. The excitement, and let's face it, sheer panic of the assault by the angry hippo had meant I'd lost focus on our relative position on the river. I knew these rapids existed and normally navigating them wasn't too much of a problem. Yep it could be rough, but not really dangerous if you had prepared to ride them out.

Of course the last thing we were at this moment was prepared. I was hanging on to the wheel as the current sucked us onwards towards the white water. Quatermain was on the deck close to the stern trying to apply at least some sort of medical aid to Cunningham. And Rajesh? I had no idea where Rajesh had disappeared to. Which on a twenty-foot boat was a pretty good trick.

Wherever he was I didn't have time to go looking for him. We hit the first part of the white water and the boat dropped a good three feet. Before she came to rest she was caught by the swirling water and driven onwards heading towards a collection of rocks off to port. I heaved on the wheel, and suddenly the tiller bit and we were pulled back into midstream. Even though we were back in the main current we were still being buffeted from side to side. Water was spraying up and over the sides and spraying into our faces making it even more difficult for me to steer a course through the rocks.

As I fought the wheel I felt the boat's movements getting more and more sluggish as if she was carrying more weight. On one short straight stretch I took the risk of taking my eyes off our erratic course and spared a second to glance down. It left me with a sinking feeling. Literally.

My feet and ankles were covered in water. There was no doubt about it; the *Lucky Lucy* was taking on water. The hits from the hippo must have compromised her structural integrity. Even if we made it through the rapids we weren't going any further.

"Get ready to go overboard," I shouted without looking back, hoping that everyone heard.

Almost immediately I felt a firm hand on my shoulder, and Quatermain's calm authoritative voice. "When we hit that next calm pool we all go. Including you."

He needn't have worried. I may have prized the *Lucky Lucy*, and she was my only source of income, but I'd never believed in that rubbish about a Captain going down with his ship.

The *Lucy* jumped forward between two rushing stream of water and settled into the clear flat pool between two rapids. I didn't hesitate. I let go of the wheel, and headed over the side.

As I surfaced I watched my livelihood disappear as she once again was caught by the current, but with no hand at the wheel to guide her destiny, was dashed to splinters on the next set of rocks.

But there was no time to grieve, I looked around and spotted Quatermain swimming to shore pulling the semi-conscious Cunningham along with him. Where the older man got his strength and stamina I'll never know. I started to follow them and as I looked over to get my line of sight was amazed to see Rajesh already stood on the riverbank waving us ashore. And neatly bundled at his feet were several of the packs from the *Lucy*. I can only think that as soon as he'd handed over the wheel to me he'd started collecting things together in case we needed to abandon ship, and that he had been the first over the side with the packs. Probably even before I'd shouted anything.

I was the last to reach shore and by the time I pulled myself out of the water it was plain to see that Rajesh and Quatermain were deep in discussion about our next move.

"Now what?" I asked. "We've no boat, and we are a couple of days away from where we planned to come ashore."

"Simple," said Quatermain, "now we start walking."

*"Quatermain...pulling...Cunningham along..."*

Spiders. I hate spiders. I guess it's one of the reasons I liked spending most of my time on the river. You don't get a lot of spiders on the water. On the other hand, the jungle is infested with them. Spiders of all sizes, and differing degrees of nastiness. It didn't take long for my discomfort around arachnids to become apparent to my traveling companions.

The three of them would happily brush off any that landed on their clothing, or push the way through any hanging web that barred our path without a second thought. The crunch of a carapace under their boots was as unremarkable as the breaking of a twig. But for me, each step deeper into the jungle became an increasing exercise in self-control.

At first Quatermain walked alongside me and attempted to point out the various different types we encountered. Imparting much of his knowledge and jungle craft about which ones were harmless, the vast majority it must be pointed out fell into this category, and which to avoid. But at the end of the day to me a spider was still a spider, and I didn't care to be around any of them.

This was not an enviable position to be in knowing that we had several days hard walking ahead of us before we reached our original path. Or at least that's what I assumed we were doing. As we set up camp on the evening of our second day in the jungle I noticed Quatermain and Rajesh were once again deep in conversation about something. From my vantage point, on a spider-free rock about twenty yards distant from them, the exchange seemed quite animated and accompanied by several bouts of arm waving and pointing.

"What's the flap about?" asked Sergeant Cunningham as he walked up to stand by my rocky retreat. He'd been busy hacking out a few feet of jungle undergrowth to make space for a temporary bivouac.

"No idea," I said, "but from the look of those gestures I think we're lost."

"Don't be ridiculous."

"I'm not being ridiculous. I've seen enough 'we're lost' arguments in my day to recognize what all that arm waving means."

"Quatermain wouldn't get lost, he's the best tracker and hunter in Africa."

"As much as we both admire the man, you can't always believe the stories. Even legends can get lost in this green hell."

Before the discussion could go any further, it was halted by the sight of Quatermain gesturing back in our direction, rapidly followed by him leaving Rajesh's side and heading towards my rocky sanctuary. "I guess we are about to find out the subject of their discourse first hand."

"Monsieur Negreau," Quatermain approached my rock, "may I be permitted to borrow the compass you were bequeathed?"

"Certainly," I responded. I must admit I'd almost forgotten about it and the other contents of the drawstring bag, which I'd attached to my belt after Rajesh had carried it ashore. Why he had seen fit to save it from the sinking boat was beyond me, but he had, and I was grateful for it, as little else of my former life now remained.

As Quatermain headed back to join Rajesh, I couldn't resist a quick jibe at Cunningham. "See. Lost. I told you so."

"I still don't believe it," he countered, "Come on, let's join them and find out what's going on."

Curiosity overcame my reluctance to step onto the jungle floor again, so I clambered down from my rock and joined Cunningham as he headed off to join our companions. As we reached them we overheard Rajesh say "I concede that we are headed in the direction to meet the path we originally mapped out." At this the Sergeant nudged me in the side with his elbow, "See." he whispered in triumph.

Rajesh continued, "But if my supposition is right about Daniel, then we should divert from that plan, and this is the place to do it."

That phrase 'supposition about Daniel,' caught my attention. "What supposition," I asked?

If Rajesh or Quatermain heard my question, they both chose to ignore it.

"Ah, Daniel." Rajesh smiled at my approach. "Can I ask did that man Karl give you any instructions when he presented you with his various gifts?"

"None that I recall."

"A shame," Rajesh sighed, "in that case we will have to trust to our own judgment and instinct."

"Instinct about what?" I asked.

"Do you recall the route we discussed?" Rajesh's question was directed more at Cunningham than myself.

"Yes, Sir." Cunningham's response was the first real military reaction I'd seen from him since our dip in the river a few days before. It was if the question had been more of an order from a superior officer than a request. "Down river in Monsieur Negreau's boat for four days to the designated landing site, then a three day march due east till we encounter the foot hills of a mountain range."

"And then?" asked Rajesh.

"You were never specific about that point, Sir."

"I wasn't, was I?" Rajesh smiled, "How remiss of me."

"I guess this is where I come in to the equation." Quatermain chipped in. "There are stories about a pass through the mountains that the elephants use. A way to the graveyard."

"Surely the elephants' graveyard is a myth." I said.

"It may be, Daniel. But as I've heard you say, most myths and stories have some grounding in truth."

"Touché." I conceded.

"The story talks of an elephant path that lies between two peaks, but that it can only be found when looking at the peaks from a particular angle and direction. The problem being that no one knows exactly what point that is."

"Until now." added Rajesh with a note of excitement in his voice.

"We still don't know for certain." cautioned Quatermain.

"I'm positive, and Daniel can help us prove it."

"Me?" I exclaimed, "How?"

Rajesh put his arm around my shoulder, which as he was several inches shorter than I proved to be something of a stretch, and led me to the point on the edge of the clearing where he and Quatermain had had their earlier arm waving contest. "What do you see?"

"Trees. Just more jungle."

"Raise your sight dear boy," He put his hand under my chin and gently tipped my head back until I was looking through a gap in the tree canopy. I could just make out several peaks of a distant mountain range. "Is that what we were heading for?"

"I believe so." Rajesh nodded, "But there's more. Look closely along the ridge line, what do you see."

"A range of peaks."

"Correct. Our pathway through."

"How do you know that?" I asked, "there's a whole line of them, even if that is the right area, how do you know which pair to head for?"

"That is where this comes in." He held up Karl's battered compass, which he must have obtained from Quatermain. "Look."

I looked down at the dial in front of me. The needle had swung away from its normal position, and instead of showing the direction of magnetic North was now resolutely pointing in the direction of the distant mountain range.

"Peculiar." I muttered.

"It is said the mountain range we seek is so rich with iron ore that it will deflect a compass." continued Rajesh.

"But that doesn't prove anything," I said, "This piece of junk is hardly reliable."

"My point, exactly." said Quatermain. "We should continue on our original planned route. Cutting through the jungle based on that evidence would be foolish."

Rajesh just smiled. "Daniel, how tall are you in comparison to the man you called Karl?"

"We were about the same height I guess, give or take half an inch."

"I thought so. Here, take the compass and hold it up to your eye and sight along the needle to the ridge line."

It seemed like a strange request, but as he was paying the bills I decided to acquiesce. "What do you see?"

"The same as before. Just the top of the mountain range."

"Look closer at the compass."

"Hang on. That's strange."

"What is?" asked Cunningham.

Unsure of what I'd just seen, I dropped the compass down, rubbed my eyes to clear them, and then returned the beaten up navigation aid to my eye line.

Sure enough the two sets of scratches on the casing rim lined up with two of the peaks on the distant ridgeline.

I moved the compass left and right scanning across the top of the mountain range again. None of the other peaks lined up. "I'll be damned."

I explained to the others what I'd seen. Rajesh was delighted. Cunningham seemed frankly disinterested, while Quatermain remained somewhat skeptical.

"Well gentlemen it seems that thanks to Daniel we have identified the entrance to the pass, now all we have to do is get there. I suggest that we all get some rest, as tomorrow we head off in a new direction."

If I'd thought the jungle trek to date had been less than ideal, in retrospect it was a walk in the park compared with this stage of our journey. As soon as we changed direction the jungle seemed to close in on us, almost as if it was trying to protect its secrets by making it almost impossible the make forward progress. The foliage became denser, the trees closer together, making it impossible to see the ridge we were aiming for from the jungle floor. We had to rely on instinct. Luckily the instinct we were relying on was Allan Quatermain's.

Progress could only be made by hacking our way through walls of foliage, creepers, and vines with machetes. A slow and tiresome way to travel. I'm not sure how far we hacked our way through the jungle on the first day, but I'm sure that despite our combined efforts it was less than a mile. Quatermain directed we should stop at a small clearing, (I say clearing, but it was just enough clear space for the four of us to stand next to each other). Without a word Quatermain started climbing a nearby tree in what I assumed was an attempt to reach the tree canopy and set his sights on our intended destination. He had also taken Karl's strange compass with him. After what seemed like an interminable wait, which was probably in fact only about a quarter of an hour, Quatermain suddenly reappeared in the clearing stepping out of the jungle ahead of us.

"Good God, where did you come from?" I asked, startled by his re-appearance from this unexpected direction.

"There's a trail." he answered, "it's old and very faint, but it's there. I hadn't seen it from the ground, but from up in the canopy it's just about visible."

"A trail from what?" asked Rajesh, "Surely not elephants, they wouldn't push through foliage this thick."

"No, not elephants." Quatermain agreed.

"Then what?" asked Cunningham.

"I'm not sure," for the first time since I'd met him I heard a note of uncertainty and puzzlement in Quatermain's voice. "At first I thought it was apes, but a family of apes would have left more damage behind and the trail would have been clearer."

"A solitary ape then?" I suggested.

"You may be right, Daniel." Quatermain said, "but the span between signs of its passage are of an extraordinary length making it taller than any ape I have encountered before. However they do provide a visual trial that points in the same direction that we are pursuing. I was able to work my way over to one of the marks, then climb down and follow my passage back to you here. Now I know what to look for, the subtle signs made by this creature's passage, we can follow and stay true to our path."

We had no choice now but to trust in Quatermain, for he was the only one among us who had the skill and experience to seek out the signs this strange ape (if that's what it was) had left behind. He did try and point out the signs to the other members of the party, and we would nod our heads, but if truth be told none of us saw the jungle the same way that Quatermain did. For him the slightest indentation in the floor, the bent branch, or broke vine was as clear as a direction post on the King's highway.

Now we had a clear direction to follow, aligned with a sense of purpose our rate of progress increased. We soon set to a rhythm, taking turns at the vanguard of our little troop to hack away at the foliage. The next three days seemed to pass in a haze as we focused solely on the task ahead, and when Quatermain descended from his daily trip to the tree canopy we were delighted to hear his news that we would break through the jungle's edge and reach the foothills of the mountain range within the next twenty four hours if we maintained our current pace.

Quatermain's estimate proved to be accurate. For at approximately midday the following day, as I was taking point at hacking our way through the undergrowth, one swing of my machete meet less resistance than I had been used to on the march so far.

"Whoa," my startled reaction rang out, bring my colleagues to my side.

"What is it?" asked Cunningham.

"The machete went straight through," I explained, "I think we at have reached the edge of the jungle."

"Well let's find out shall we?" said Cunningham as he started pulling at the vines and foliage in front to us.

I stepped to one side so not to hit him with my blade, and continued hacking away at the greenery around us. Sure enough between the two of us we quickly created an opening through which we could clearly see the mountain range that was our destination. Between them and us seemed to lay a mix of scrub land and grassy plain not more than half a mile across. On beholding such a welcome sight, the Sergeant and I redoubled our efforts and soon we had opened up a passage large enough for the four of us to step through. The relief amongst our party was almost palpable.

"Good work, Daniel," Quatermain slapped me on my shoulders.

"Bravo, Mr. Negreau." added Rajesh, in a tone that bordered on patronizing.

After the round of congratulations, we walked a few feet away from the jungle edge, and settled down in to a shaded culvert to make ourselves a meal and relax for the rest of the day. The respite was both well deserved and welcome. For the first time since the capsize of my boat, we felt at ease. Surely the short passage to the foot of the mountains would be the easiest part of the journey, and we felt the need to prepare ourselves for the climb to follow.

We spent the afternoon, as men tend to, trying to outdo each other in the telling of yarns. Sergeant Cunningham was more than happy to regale us with tales of his regiment's accomplishments in various conflicts, as well as a few tales of his own experiences in battle. Rajesh regaled us with stories of learning to train Indian elephants, and described at length the differences between the Indian pachyderm and its distant cousin to be found roaming the Dark Continent. Although on reflection he didn't reveal anything about how or why he came to be in Africa. Allan Quatermain proved to be a reluctant celebrity, but after much cajoling he did offer a few tales of his various adventures as an elephant hunter. Rumors around tales of his other adventures he refused to confirm or acknowledge much to my frustration. As for myself, listening to my three companions made me feel somewhat unworthy of their fellowship. For what was I but a simple riverboat trader with no real adventure in my life?

Quatermain sensed my reluctance and pushed me to tell how I had ended up in Africa. It was a small tale to offer in comparison to the others, but I obliged him.

"I have always been a product of the water trade. My father, and his before him, plied their trade as bargemen and river pilots on the St. Lawrence, aiding ships of various size and nationality make berth in the city of Montreal, Canada. On the side they also helped those whose water borne commerce was a little less legal. Smugglers.

"I joined my father on the river at the age of seven, where my schooling became that of the waterman, learning to read the ebb and flow of the St. Lawrence well before I could read my letters.

"As I grew older my father started to leave me to my own devices when he didn't need me on his barges, so I began to hire myself out to other boatmen, or traders, who could use my talents. And so it was at the age of fourteen I found myself hired by three gentlemen to help them navigate their way to a particular secluded landing place just down river from the city, and the careful eye of the customs authorities. Or so we thought. On landing at the designated spot we found several customs officers awaiting our arrival. The cargo of contraband was seized and the three men arrested. The custom agents let me go, citing my young age, and believing that I knew nothing about the smuggling. Which was true up to a point. I knew that the men were smugglers, but not what it was they were transporting. However, the arrested men took my release as proof that I had been in the employ of the customs men and betrayed them.

"Although I was well below the age of majority, I was now a marked man, and my usefulness to my father's business non-existent.

"In order to preserve his business, and my skin, (And I believe that was the correct order of his priorities), he sent me south to America. To the port of Baltimore in fact, where some distant relations lived.

"After arriving at the city I tried to avoid falling into the same line of work, but found myself drawn inexorably back to the water. I eventually secured employment working the water taxi that ferried residents and businessmen between the city's harbor and the district known as Fell's Point. Among my regular passengers was a man perhaps in his late forties or early fifties who started to converse with me, something no one else did. I discovered he was a professor at the local university, while he persuaded me to tell my tale. On discovering my lack of any formal education he declared that a boy as obviously intelligent as myself (the first time anyone had applied that descriptor to me) should receive some schooling. He invited me to visit his home, and over the course of numerous visits he taught me to read, and write, as well as instilling in me an understanding of figures and business.

"But above all, he sparked my interest in Africa. The library of his house, in which he conducted my lessons, was lined with numerous books on the Dark Continent. After I discovered the joy of reading, I would often pull books on various aspects of Africa from the shelves when he had occasion to leave the room. One day his young daughter, who I had hadn't seen in the house previously, discovered me with her father's books.

"Instead of throwing me out for my presumption, the Professor encouraged my behavior, and interest in Africa. It soon became the sole subject of discourse between us.

"After a few years of splitting my time between working the water taxi, and studying with the professor, I knew I had come to the point where I needed to branch out and make my own way in the world. About a week after making this declaration, the Professor amazed me by presenting me with the gift of a paid passage to Cape Town and some seed money for me to make my own way in this new continent.

"I used the money to travel up the coast until I found a suitable spot, and there started my riverboat business. Which is where you gentlemen discovered me. I may not have made a fortune, but I was content with my life. Of course it seems that now destiny has decided to take me along yet another path."

"An excellent story, Daniel." Quatermain remarked after I concluded my narrative, "And you may be correct, who knows what destiny awaits any of us?"

After I had finished my tale, he settled down for the night to get some rest, with a small fire kept burning to ward off any wild animals and the seemingly indefatigable Quatermain agreeing to stand watch.

Despite the hardness of the ground, it was good to stretch out under an open sky again rather than the claustrophobic ever present tree canopy. I was soon soundly asleep.

What it was that woke me, I'm not sure, but I snapped awake. Looking round I saw that everyone else was awake too.

"What is it?" I asked.

"Be quiet." hissed Cunningham who had been sleeping alongside me. He nodded towards to southern most point of the culvert where Rajesh and Quatermain were both crouched intently listening.

The African night is never totally silent; depending on where you are there is always something making a noise, animal or insect. The sound that suddenly split the night was unlike any animal or insect I had ever heard before.

It was primal. Almost as if something, or someone's, soul had been ripped from their body.

"My God!" my exclamation was involuntary.

"There was no God involved in that." said Rajesh.

Then the night fell silent. An unnatural silence. Whatever that was, had not only sacred us, it had silenced all the natural life in the area. It was the most monstrous sound I had ever heard.

No one spoke for what seemed like an eternity, but was probably only a minute or so. Then the silence was broken by a voice, which I was surprised to realize was my own.

"What now?" My voice was a harsh whisper.

"We go back to sleep." Quatermain replied. "Whatever that was, it's is beyond any help we may offer. We need the rest. Go back to sleep."

I don't know if the others slept, but I didn't. I lay on my back staring at the stars until they disappeared as the sky brightened. That horrible sound replaying itself in my mind over and over again. I hoped, for its own sake, that whatever had made that sound was dead.

It wasn't.

We came across it about two hours into our morning march across the scrubland. We had decided to cross that plain as quickly as possible to try and put the horror of the night behind us. So Sergeant Cunningham had declared that we should proceed at a forced march pace.

We saw it as he crested a small rise. There in front of use was a sight I will never forget.

Excuse my pause in the narrative; even after all these years the image in my mind still gives me the shivers. But I must carry on for what awaited us that morning is vital to the telling of the rest of the tale to come.

✿ ✿ ✿

Ahead of us the ground was moving. Not like in an earthquake, but shimmering and pulsating in waves as if it was alive and going through a series of convulsions. As we drew nearer the reason for the effect became clear, a patch of ground about ten feet by four was covered in spiders. The largest meanest looking spiders I have ever seen. I will admit that given my feelings towards arachnids the sight made me shudder to my core, but what I perceived next made me vomit on the spot.

For the mass of spiders were moving in a pattern, and the shape that their movements drew on that horrific plain was that of a man. There was someone underneath that mass of skittering horror.

At the same time that my gag reflex kicked in, Allan Quatermain also reacted, although his actions were more humane and heroic than mine. He strode into the mass. Spiders started to skitter and climb over his boots and up his legs, but he paid them no heed. As he reached the head of the submerged man he leant down and placed his hand among the sea of arachnids pushing them aside to reveal the countenance of the man beneath the waves.

"He's still alive!" Quatermain shouted, "but only just." He looked back straight at Sergeant Cunningham. "Make a torch, burn the creatures off. I'll keep the head clear." and with that he returned to the seemingly hopeless task of beating back the onslaught of spiders.

Cunningham grabbed a couple of rags from our packs, quickly tied them around some branches pulled from scrubland brushes. He made three such devices, then setting light to the rags gave one to Rajesh and myself (having stopped retching up the meager contents of my stomach), with instructions to "Burn the bastards. Get them off him."

It was a task I set to with a certain relish, I will admit. We all went at with a combination of gusto and abandon, not caring too much about the poor wretch under the spiders. A burn would be little on top of what he must already be suffering.

The torches worked well enough. Those spiders that weren't burned were scared off by the flames and heat and scuttled away to the undergrowth or returned to various holes in the ground.

*"Make a torch, burn the creatures off!"*

When the last live one disappeared we set to the task of removing the roasted carapaces of those that hadn't escaped the flames.

What was revealed underneath was the saddest example of humanity I had ever seen. He was a large man; over six feet and well muscled. He had been staked out on the plains floor, stripped naked and left to the denizens of the wild to be eaten alive. But what nauseated me most was his left arm.

The skin had been carefully peeled off his arm from the shoulder to the wrist, probably while he was fully conscious. This must have been the cause of the unholy scream the night before.

"Why would they do that?" The question escaped from by dry vomit covered lips.

"The spiders." Quatermain responded. "The blood and muscle would be a tempting meal. It was a way to invite them to feast first. A slower, more painful death for the victim than being torn apart by a big cat."

"How could he still be alive after that?"

"His size." Cunningham answered my question, "A smaller man wouldn't have lasted as long."

"Last night. You said...." I stared accusingly at Quatermain. "We could have..." the accusation hung unfinished in the air between us.

"Now is not the time." Rajesh interjected. "We must help this man."

"I'll do it." Cunningham stepped forward with his cocked service revolver in his hand. He placed the barrel against the temple of the poor victim.

His finger tightened as he started to squeeze, just as he reached the trigger's pressure point Quatermain shoved him aside with a violent shove. The shot went wide of the man's head and thudded into the soil a few inches away.

"What the?" Cunningham has outraged.

"As Daniel pointed out," Quatermain replied, "I could have saved this man. He is my responsibility."

"We can't take him with us. He needs extensive medical aid. He is beyond help." Cunningham countered.

"I can save him." Quatermain was undaunted.

"Daniel stand by with one of those torches, and when I direct you, place it where I point."

Quatermain set to with his knife cutting the vine rope bonds that held the man to the stakes. He then put out his hand for the machete that had helped us hack our way through the jungle. Without comment Rajesh handed it over, then stepped forward and grabbed the man's skinned left arm at the wrist and pulled it taught. Quatermain placed one foot on the man's chest just below the collarbone to steady the body.

We swung the machete with all his might. With the third blow Rajesh fell backwards as the arm separated at a point a couple of inches below its top ball joint where it attaches to the shoulder. As he did so, Quatermain yelled "Now, Daniel!" and I drove the flaming torch into the wound, cauterizing it. The smell of burning flesh assailing my nostrils.

The pain and shock of the impromptu amputation caused our patient to scream again, but this time it was more a scream of relief; if such a thing is possible.

With the operation over, Quatermain set to using what few salves and soothing ointments we had in our packs to dress the numerous bites that covered the rest of the man's body. His remaining flesh was a veritable mass of sores, bites, and swelling, so numerous as to make him unrecognizable. In fact it was even difficult to determine if he was white or colored such was the devastation wrought by the spiders.

As Quatermain worked, the man stated to emit small noises as if waking from his horror. Rajesh and I were near his head as we continued to dress the stump of his arm and shoulder. We heard what sounded like a word being repeated.

Rajesh leaned closer to listen. After the next utterance he exclaimed. "Stop, Quatermain. He is beyond saving. He pleads for mercy."

The man spoke again. This time I listened. He said but a single word.

"It's not 'mercy,' it's 'merci.' He is saying 'thank you.'" And at that point I knew who the unfortunate victim was.

"It's the Frenchman!"

Ankole-Watusi, that's what Quatermain said they were called, although to me they were just cattle. I will accept that the large eight foot span horns were more impressive than any other cattle I had seen.

Sergeant Cunningham seemed surprisingly cheered at their arrival, and even took to giving them pet names.

While Quatermain had been off in parts unknown, the Sergeant and I had set to pulling together a makeshift stretcher on which to carry the Frenchman. We made a few sorties back into the nearby jungle to source branches, vines to use as binding rope, and broad leaves to act as covers.

The combination of the military man's field experience and my river borne knowledge of ropes we quickly put together a stout frame over which we wove a lattice of vines and fronds to provide a supportive, but flexible base on which to rest the injured man. Over his naked, brutalized body we placed a combination of leaves and what spare blankets we had between us. In this condition we awaited the return of Quatermain whilst doing what we could to soothe the troubled mind and body of the ravaged Frenchman. The poor man see-sawed between delirium and a stupor that left him oblivious to the world and his pain. Thankfully he spent the majority of his time in this latter condition.

Presently Quatermain appeared from behind a small hillock to the west of us leading two specimens of the aforementioned cattle. He offered no explanation as to where, or how, he had obtained them; nor did we inquire.

In fact the only statement from Quatermain was that we should return to the jungle's edge to find longer branches with which to construct an A-frame. Once built this frame was lashed to one of the beasts so that it trailed behind in such a way that the makeshift stretcher could be rested on top, making the transport of our wounded man easier.

With this temporary ambulance in position we started our march towards the foothills. Quatermain lead the way, Cunningham guided the beast of burden, Rajesh taking charge of the extra beast, while I walked alongside the stretcher listening in case our patient muttered anything else in his mother tongue. Even if he did I'm not sure how much use I would have been. I may have been born and raised in Montreal, but I wasn't much of a Francophile and had little to do with the French-speaking residents of the city. I hadn't heard the language spoken on a regular basis since my boyhood, and had never really spoken it beyond a word or two. But even this little exposure was more than anyone else in our party, so the task of conversing with the Frenchman, if he ever woke, fell to me.

As we reached the edge of the foothills, the ground changed from grass and scrub to rocks and lose shale. The going got harder and our pace slowed. Even so I was surprised at the end of the day to look back over our path and see how far we had climbed. As we set camp, Quatermain again disappeared on the premise of scouting ahead to determine the following day's route. He returned an hour later with news that there appeared to be a flat wide plateau between us and the ridgeline we were aiming for. A good place to rest, and hopefully find water and small animals with which to replenish our supplies. For both were starting to dwindle, and we had less than three days left at our current rate of consumption. With an extra mouth to now keep nourished, it may not even last that long. We were working on the unspoken hope that whatever was over that ridge would provide the bounty we needed, if the plateau met Quatermain's expectations, so much the better.

We reached it around mid-afternoon, and were less than impressed by what we saw. While the plateau was wide and flat enough to provide a respite from the continuous climb of the last few days, there was no way it resembled the verdant respite we had all been hoping for. The surface was covered with as much shale and rocks as the slopes below it. A logical observation of course, but to a group of hungry, thirsty, tired men still a disappointment.

A disappointment compounded by the fact we suddenly found ourselves surrounded by a dozen or more tribesmen carrying large spears, the majority of which were clearly pointed in our direction with apparent malicious intent.

As the circle of encroaching natives drew tighter around us Cunningham's hand slowly moved towards his the service revolver at his side. Quatermain, stood slightly in front and to one side of the military man, must have either caught the movement with his peripheral vision, or, more likely, sensed it. Whatever the cause he turned around to face Cunningham and quickly raised his hand, palm out. "No!" it was a clear and curt command.

I suddenly realized that in turning around to thwart Cunningham's reaction, Quatermain had exposed his back to the natives. My mouth started to form the words to warn him of his precarious position, but before I could say anything he repositioned his own hand to place a finger over his lips in a silent command for us to remain quiet.

And so it was we remained in a silent impasse. A strange frozen tableau on this rocky escarpment, five civilized men surrounded by denizens of the Dark Continent. Both groups with the means to destroy each other, but neither moving.

Slowly Quatermain lowered his hand from his face and gradually drew his arms out wide to indicate that he held no weapons. He then rotated around to face the spear points. Looking around the circle of faces he settled on one man and then spoke slowly and clearly, making sure to enunciate every syllable. "Tomasu boet."

I had no idea what the words meant at that point, but they had the desired effect. They didn't kill us.

Although I still wasn't sure if that course of action had been abandoned, or merely postponed in their minds.

"Keep your weapons holstered," ordered Quatermain, "and follow my lead." So saying he stepped towards the man he had obviously decided was the de facto leader of this group. As he approached the man, Quatermain spread his arms wide, glancing back over his shoulder at us, he nodded slightly. Following his lead we all took up the same posture. The lead tribesman suddenly uttered a guttural sound which I think was a close approximation of a laugh, slapped Quatermain's arms down with a wide downward swing of his own powerful arms, and then pointed in a direction back over his shoulder.

"I guess we follow," grumbled Cunningham, who was exhibiting visible mistrust in our new, unasked for, guides.

And so our strange party set off, the natives leading us to a path off the ridge. We made perhaps the strangest column yet seen in those parts. At our head were Quatermain and the native he had selected as the leader. The two appeared to be conversing by a series of guttural sounds and hand gestures, which made no sense to me. Behind them another native led the animal on which the Frenchman's makeshift stretcher was mounted. Cunningham walked in step with him, his hand resting on the base of the animals' neck as if giving it silent encouragement to pull its heavy load. Next came Rajesh and myself. Neither of us spoke. But we did exchange glances at the two warriors that walked alongside, a silent indication that we both realized that we were in fact under guard. Behind us came the remaining two warriors leading the second animal, which had been loaded with all our packs and the supplies we'd foraged from the jungle. During the loading I had once more managed to take possession of my pouch and hidden it inside my shirt, away from the prying eyes of the natives.

Despite the unspoken misgivings of the Indian and myself, the journey progressed without incident. Twice a day we stopped for break. In the evenings the natives made camp and set fires. Two of them would disappear and return shortly with some small animal or other which was subsequently roasted on the fires. I'm never sure what it was we ate over those few days, but the meat was always succulent, and after our meager rations to date, they tasted as good as the best Sunday roast.

So it was that our party drifted towards a tentative sense of companionship with our guides, for this is how I'd come to now think of them. Especially between Cunningham and the native who tended the cattle. The two seemed to share a surprising common interest in the bovines' welfare.

About mid-morning of the fourth day of our march, we crested a rise in the path. The sight that lay before us halted the four civilized men in the tracks.

"My God Almighty!" the exclamation was Quatermain's. Surprising on two fronts; one in that I had never heard him swear or blaspheme, and secondly I would have thought he had encountered everything there was to see in Africa by this point. The fact that he was as stunned as the rest of us was a testament to what lay before us. I have never been a man of faith, and I must confess it's not something I'd ever considered, but my first thought on seeing the vista that opened up before us was, this must be what Eden looked like. For what lay before us truly looked like paradise. The valley was rich in verdant grasslands, and plant life. Trees were abundant enough to provide shelter, but not encroaching like the jungle we had not long left. They also appeared, even at this distance, heavy with fruit. On the fields between them roamed many head of cattle similar to the ones that accompanied us. Along the valley floor ran a wide river; whose free flowing water was the calmest and clearest I'd ever seen in Africa. Judging from the activity of the men in the small coracle type boats on its surface I guessed it was also abundant in fish.

Nestled in a curve of the river we could discern a village, its huts and low buildings apparently arranged around a central square from which we could see smoke rising from several fire pits. Unlike many native villages, this one did not lie behind a protective balustrade wall, but was open to the surrounding country, apparently allowing easy access for man and beast. From this I surmised that predatory animals were also unknown in his valley.

What kept this nirvana from the ravages of the jungle around it were the mountain ranges behind and to the side that sheltered the valley from the worst ravages of weather, yet promoted its temperate climate, and on the fourth side the one obstacle that now lay directly in our path; a massive ravine.

The aforementioned river, on reaching the edge of the valley, overflowed a cliff edge and tumbled into the ravine from such a height that the water plume never reached the bottom, instead turning into a continuous mist. Across this misty crevasse stretched the only method of ingress into the valley, a bridge constructed of rope vines, with a deck of roughly hewn tree trunks lashed together.

As we approached the crossing I began to view the structure with more and more uncertainty, for the closer we got, the more I could see what I had thought was a solid construction was swaying to and fro in the winds that raced through the ravine. Those same winds would also pick up the mist from the waterfall, often blowing them over the bridge rendering its surface slick with water.

I began to have my doubts as to its safety.

Perhaps I was alone in such fears, for Quatermain and his native companion strode onto the swaying slippery deck without breaking stride. They seemed as calm as if they we walking in midday conversation along the Thames Embankment. Given such display of confidence it would have seemed churlish not to follow. The driver of the first beast, in conjunction with Cunningham, persuaded the animal to join them on the bridge and they slowly made their way forward dragging their burden behind them. The bouncing of the A-frame structure across the uneven surface caused the recumbent Frenchman to moan with each jolt of the stretcher.

As we approached the bridge, Rajesh stopped and looked at me. An expression of fear on his face. "Daniel," his voice almost quivered, "I have never been much for heights. In fact I usually go out of my way to avoid them."

"What of the mountain climb?" I asked.

"I could focus on the wall by my side, it helped give some relief from the vertigo. But this," he gestured at the bridge," is open to the elements. I'm not sure I can make it."

"Of course you can," and I held out my hand towards him. The short Indian took the proffered hand, and we stepped onto the bridge.

The combination of the rounded surface of the tree trunks, the mist, and the swaying made it feel treacherous. A combination that did little to sooth my companion's nerves. The worse part was the swaying. The rhythm from the footsteps of six men and the oxen had started a swing that seemed to increase in oscillation with each step. I instructed Rajesh to focus on a fixed point at the end of the crossing in the hope that his senses would ignore both the height and movement of our crossing. This technique seemed to work well for the first half of the crossing. The first inclination of its failure was a muted sob from my side.

As soon as I looked around I knew that Rajesh was in trouble. His gaze had shifted and was now firmly fixed downwards at the shifting deck beneath our feet. The advice about not looking down when crossing over a chasm like this one might be something of a cliché, but it has value.

"Look up." I commanded.

"I can't" he muttered, and in that instant also let go of my steadying hand. Without my grip he started to sway in concert with the bridge's oscillations. The inevitable happened. Rajesh started to fall away from me, and instead of making a grab for me; he lunged out in the opposite direction trying to anchor himself on one of the bridge's vine ropes.

He missed. And without a sound the small Indian disappeared over the side into the ravine below.

Instinctively I lunged after him in what I already knew was a futile attempt to save him. As I reached the edge of the bridge and was about to join Rajesh, my momentum was brought to an abrupt stop by a firm grip on my belt. I teetered on the edge of oblivion for a few seconds before being pulled back onto the relative safety of the slick surfaced swaying bridge. I felt the securing grip from behind me loosen as I regained my footing. Turning round I was relieved to see Allan Quatermain stood in front of me. But this was a different Quatermain than I'd seen to date.

For now the man looked like the legend I had imagined. Although I knew he was in his fifties, he wasn't a man who let age define him. Rather he defied his age. While not particularly large of stature, he seemed to me to be larger than life. His skin was browned and toughened by his years in the sun. During our brief acquaintance he had habitually worn a wide brimmed hat to shield his face and neck from the ravages of the sun. How he had held on to it during our travails, I had no idea. But at this moment it seemed to fit him as well as a knight's helmet, while his tatty tan shirt, patched trousers, and worn boots took on the sheen of golden armor. But the one thing I remember from that moment were the eyes. The eyes of a born predator, a warrior, a man to obey, a man to follow into the jaws of hell if he demanded it.

He only spoke one word to me. "Move."

The rest of the crossing occurred without incident, but as we continued our journey towards the village, the beauty of our surroundings was lost on me. My mind became obsessed with Rajesh and the accident on the bridge. I had hardly spoken to the Indian during our journey so far. As I mentioned before the man talked a lot, but actually said very little. As a consequence I had started to mentally push his twittering to the back of my mind, taking little notice of his chatter. So I made no real attempt to get to know him; yet now I felt his loss deeply. In many ways I began to feel that his death had been my responsibility. With each step we took through paradise, my gloom and despondency deepened.

About an hour after stepping off the bridge we entered the village and made our way to the central area, where we were soon surrounded by a gaggle of curious villagers. And what a strange sight we must have been:

the elephant hunter and the military man accompanied by a morose grieving river rat and a delirious giant of a man half eaten alive by spiders.

Our audience initially comprised a mix of curious women and inquisitive children. The women, both young and old, hung back observing us from a safe distance, chattering away while pointing at the curiosities before them. A few of the children ventured forward and poked at the recumbent form on the stretcher behind the horned cattle. Unsure of what form of man lay before them they used sticks rather than make physical contact, each contact provoking a moan from the poor battered Frenchman. This response prompted a series of giggles from the children, encouraging more of them to creep forward, sticks in hand.

I was expecting the warriors who had accompanied us to stop this cruel, if innocent, behavior, but none stepped forward to intercede. A glance around showed that they had all disappeared leaving us to the attentions of the curious women and children.

The air was suddenly filled with a strange cry. It was a combination of a scream, and yodel, punctuated with a series of rhythmic guttural clicks.

I was astonished to discover that the source of the sound was none other than Quatermain himself. I had no idea what the cry meant, but it sounded like a challenge to me. Sergeant Cunningham must have come to the same conclusion, as he grabbed Quatermain's shoulders and spun him around with a hissed "What are you doing? You'll get us killed."

"No matter what you see next," Quatermain responded in a smooth modulated voice, "Stay calm."

It wasn't easy to follow his advice, for out of the gaps between the huts appeared a host of warriors, all with a fierce look on their faces, and murder in their eyes. All were in full battle dress and carried body length shields covered with hide, presumably from the cattle we'd seen, and a variety of weapons, knives, curved swords, arrows, lances etc. chief amongst was a staff pike of about six feet in length. Both Cunningham and I scanned the advancing crowd trying to recognize the warriors that had accompanied us from the escarpment and across the bridge, desperate to locate anything that might be a friendly face. But they all looked the same; there was no succor to be found here. Slowly, inexorably they approached and the circle grew tighter. Cunningham and I stood back to back determined to protect each other, in what we both knew would be a futile attempt to ward off our impending doom. Quatermain stood apart from us, seemingly oblivious to our fate.

The lead warriors in the host were close enough that they could have used the pikes to reach out and touch us, when Quatermain repeated the guttural clicking sound. The warriors stopped. For several heart beats not a sound passed. It was utter silence, I didn't even hear the background chatter of the village, nor the birdsong or animal sounds from the valley floor.

We all just stood and stared at each other.

The silence was broken by another cry, but this time it didn't come from Quatermain, but rather from a point somewhere behind the assembled warriors. Slowly the warriors lined up in front of Quatermain parted, and through their ranks strode the tallest example of man I have ever seen.

Whether he was the chief of this village, or its greatest warrior, I couldn't tell. Maybe he was both, for he towered over everyone, at a good seven feet in height, maybe more. His face, pockmarked with decorative scars, was held in a threatening grimace so we had a good view of his teeth, all filed to a point. In his hand he carried what looked to be a golden arrow shaft. I assumed this to be a symbolic piece of his regalia as the arrow, while fully fletched, carried no tip. He wore a headdress made from the plumage of various jungle birds, but little else. Around his waist was a rope belt from which hung a knife with a long curved blade, along with the thing that most caught my attention, several shrunken heads, some of which had clearly once belonged to white men.

I watched in terror as the tall chieftain, for this was who I now assumed the giant warrior to be, walked up to within a few feet of Quatermain. The elephant hunter didn't flinch. He stood his ground, and tipping his head back to meet the giant's gaze. The two stood looking at each other. After a few seconds the chieftain titled his head back and gave another of those strange yodeling cries. Suddenly the whole village joined in his exaltation. It was at this moment I fully expected the killing blow to be delivered. For Quatermain to fall to the curved blade, and for the rest of us to be pounced upon by the surrounding host.

The giant's arms swung downward, but instead of reaching for his blade, his hands settled on Quatermain's shoulders with a firm grasp. He lifted Quatermain up off his feet until the two were eye to eye. The grimace transitioned into a broad smile, and he spoke.

"Welcome to my home Pale Hunter, it has been too long since our paths crossed."

I was stunned.

Not so much as the words he spoke, but more by his accent. For this seven foot savage, here in a hidden valley in the depths of the African

*"Welcome to my home Pale Hunter…"*

continent, spoke with the annunciation and rounded vowel sounds that were indicative of being a product of the English Public School system.

"I'm delighted to see you again, Tomasu," responded Quatermain, "but would find it easier to converse with my feet on the ground."

The chieftain, who I now knew was named Tomasu, the word we had heard Quatermain use to the tribesmen on the escarpment, lowered the older man back to terra-firma. Placed an arm around his shoulders leading him off towards the largest dwelling in the village. Quatermain stood his ground and looked back in our direction. "What about my companions? Are they also under your protecting embrace."

Tomasu looked back and regarded us as if really noticing us for the first time. "All who enter my village are under my protection. You have no reason to fear." He then pointed at the injured Frenchman on the stretcher, and called out something using the sequence of guttural clicks, that I came to recognize as the language of this tribe. As he did so several women appeared from behind the ring of warriors. "My wives will see to your wounded man, and in the mean time you and your companions must join me for a meal and regale me with the tales of your adventures so far, and the treasures that you seek. For I am sure this unworthy village is not your final destination."

That evening we ate like kings, for we feasted on the fruits of the forest and the fatted calf, all washed down with sweet ale that Tomasu claimed he had invented by introducing English brewing techniques to his tribe on his home-coming.

Tomasu confirmed what I had surmised earlier, that he had been educated in an English Public School, Eton to be exact. His father, the former chief, had become very friendly with a former colonial governor, and the official had taken it upon himself to see that his friend's son received a proper education, and so it was that the young Tomasu was dispatched to the mother country. After completing his education he had planned to study medicine, but had then received word that his father was ailing so had returned to Africa. It was in his first few months back on African soil that he and Quatermain had apparently crossed paths, but what adventure had befallen them neither would elaborate.

He had arrived back in the village just in time to spend a few hours with his father before the old chieftain's death. On his death bed the old man had made Tomasu promise to spend the rest of his days protecting the village and preserving its customs, and with that had passed him the golden broken arrow totem carried by the leader of the tribe. "Since that day," Tomasu spoke in a quiet, almost reverential tone, "I have protected both my tribe, and provided shelter and succor for any who may find their way here."

There was one aspect of his story that had piqued my curiosity, and I couldn't hold it at bay any more. "Surely you didn't look and dress like that at Eton?" I blurted out, hoping that my remark wouldn't cause offense. Instead the giant warrior laughed, "No. Apart from my prodigious height and ebony skin I was no different than any other boy at the school. This," he waved his hand over the decorative scars, and across his mouth to indicate the filed teeth, "all came after my ascension to tribal leader. They come with the position."

"What about those?" I asked pointing to the shrunken heads on his vine belt.

"Ah those. Those are part of the tradition I mentioned."

I gulped. Loudly.

"But don't worry Daniel," it is a tradition long since surpassed by more modern values of morality. "These heads have been passed down from generation to generation of chieftains, and are probably well over a hundred years old. They are symbols of an age long gone and a reminder that we shouldn't return to our barbaric past." With that he shifted his gaze back to Quatermain. "So I have told you my story, what of you and your companions Pale Hunter? For instance, the wounded man. Who is he?"

"We know little of him beyond that he is a French mercenary employed by someone who seems to hold a grudge against me, who that is, and why the vendetta, I have no idea."

"In that case, do you wish me to order my wives to desist in their care and let him die?"

For all his veneer of civilization, I mused, Tomasu could still be a savage.

"No!" Quatermain's response was adamant. "If he recovers and has any sense of gratitude, he should be able to tell us the name of his employer." I had my doubts about the Frenchman's ability to show gratitude, but I could see Quatermain's point.

"And what of you, Monsieur Negreau?" Tomasu looked in my direction, "What's your story?"

I spent the next hour recounting the details of my life that I have already shared, along with an account of our journey from my encounter with Karl and his mysterious gifts, up to our current situation.

"If you have no objection, I would like to peruse the singular gifts that this recalcitrant German bestowed on you." Tomasu's request seemed reasonable, but I looked at Quatermain for approval. He quietly nodded his assent, so I removed the pouch from under my shirt and handed it to the Chieftain.

Taking it from me with a slight bow of acknowledgment he stepped back, squatted down before us and gently opened the drawstring before spilling the contents onto the cattle skin rug in front of him.

He carefully laid them out in a line, spacing them out equally. Looking at each in turn he muttered to himself.

Then slowly he picked each up in turn, examined them more closely before passing comment. The compass elicited little response, the Parisian postcard brought a wry smile to his face, "Well this brings back some very pleasant memories," the chief smiled.

Passing over the arrow head, he picked up the ivory tusk. "So this is the catalyst for your adventure?" We nodded in confirmation. "It doesn't look that special."

"Hold it in the light," Quatermain instructed.

As the sun had long set, Tomasu stood and headed in the direction of the low burning fire in the center of the hut. As others had done before, he slowly rotated the tusk in the ambient glow. After a few seconds he issued a low appreciative whistle, a more British reaction than African. "Now I understand your quest, my friend. How could the Pale Hunter resist such a prize?"

Returning to the line of items on the rug he replaced the ivory, and picked up the arrow tip. "And then there's this. What do you know of this artifact, Monsieur Negreau?"

I was a little taken aback that he'd addressed me as his focus had seemed to be on Allan Quatermain for the last few minutes, "Noth... nothing," I stammered, "Only that I, nor anyone I've shown it to has seen that design of arrowhead before."

"And nor will they have." Tomasu said in a stern voice.

"Why are you so certain of that, my friend?" asked Quatermain.

"It is a design unique to this tribe, and one that has not been seen for many generations. Only the chiefs of the tribe are educated in its design and meaning." Tomasu lifted the arrow tip, holding it between his thumb and index finger. He slowly rotated it in the firelight as he had done with the ivory just a few moments before. For the first time we witnessed that the arrow tip emitted the same golden glow.

I was speechless. I hadn't anticipated this latest development. From the look on Quatermain's face as I glanced across to him, I suspected that this was as much of a surprise to him as it was to me.

"How did you know it would glow in that way?" Quatermain addressed Tomasu.

"I didn't, but I suspected it might." he reached behind him, picking up the ceremonial arrow shaft, "And this is the reason." With that the chieftain held the tip over the top of the shaft. He hesitated for a few seconds before pushing the two objects together. The tip slid into place, as easily as if it had always rested there, and I suspected there was a lot of truth in that supposition.

Tomasu stood, and announced with royal authority, "I shall be joining you on the rest of your quest." We didn't argue.

Suddenly it struck me that I hadn't heard a single interjection, comment from Sargeant Cunningham during this development. I looked around the chief's hut, but could see no sign of him.

Tomasu relaxed and smiled, "If you are looking for your military companion, he slipped away from our gathering at the end of the meal."

I excused myself, leaving Tomasu and Quatermain to talk of times past, and headed out in search of the Sergeant. The village was quiet, yet as I listened I heard the low murmur of voices being carried on the cool breeze that flowed along the valley floor. As I turned to try and catch which direction it originated from I caught sight of a small campfire burning low in a field just beyond the perimeter of the huts. As I approached I spotted our missing comrade squatted down among a circle of tribesmen, apparently deep in conversation. Something I knew was impossible, for Quatermain was the only member of our party to have any understanding of their strange guttural tongue.

Cunningham spotted my approach and waved for me to join him. "Ah, Daniel, come join us."

Two of the tribesmen moved to make room for me to squat between them, widening the circle. Despite the hospitality of the last few hours I must admit to still feeling on edge in such strange company. I couldn't shake off the feeling that all was not as it should be. Cunningham, however, seemed perfectly at ease and relaxed. "How are you are communicating with them?" I asked.

"The universal language of hand gestures and pictures," he pointed down to the dirt in front of him, upon which, illuminated by the fire light, I saw various squiggles that had been etched into the surface with a stick. Some looked like pictograms of cattle, both the long horned African beasts we had encountered, and the more common European style animal. Other scratches looked like a map.

Cunningham smiled and pointed at the cow-like pictograms. "These fine chaps are the herdsmen of the tribe. My family has been cattle drovers for generations. One cattleman to another. It didn't take long to find some common ground."

"And the map?" I asked.

"There are no enclosures here. The cattle wander far and wide in search of good grazing. The herdsmen wander with them, as a result they know the valley and its surrounding areas better than any one. They know the path through the peaks we seek, and what lies beyond it." With that Cunningham returned to his strange conversation with the drivers, as they continued to scratch in the dirt adding more detail to this strange map. After a while I lost interest and wandered back to the village and the hut I had been assigned, where, despite my misgivings, I soon fell into the soundest most restful sleep I'd experienced in weeks.

Early the following morning well rested and well fed, our revised party set out to continue our journey to try and resolve the riddle of the golden ivory. The Frenchman stayed behind in the village where Tomasu assured us his wounds would be treated. As he had proclaimed the night before, the imposing chieftain had now joined our party along with two of the herdsmen befriended by Cunningham. But before we ventured beyond the idyllic valley we once more paused at the edge of the gorge by the rope bridge to spend a few moments in silence to mark the loss of our former colleague.

The subsequent return crossing of the bridge was both incident free, and conducted under a gloom of silent melancholy.

Back on the escarpment, the herdsmen pointed us back on the path between the peaks, and with the direction confirmed by my compass, our spirits lifted. So it was that our party of six began the last leg of our adventure.

Apes. During the span of my life I have meet several people who seem obsessed with our simian cousins. What they often don't realize is that there really is no such thing as a typical ape. The number of types, variety, and behavior is as diverse as we homo sapiens. At the time of the adventure I'm currently recounting I was unaware of Mr. Darwin's theories of the connection between man and ape, as was everyone else in our party, but events would serve to illuminate the theory and convince me that the controversial evolutionist may have had a viable hypothesis. In fact I'm convinced that what we encountered may go even beyond what he proposed, but once again I am getting ahead of my narrative.

As promised, the two herdsmen led us to the path between the peaks. It was relatively straight forward in comparison to our journey so far, and nothing untoward befell our party or the two cattle that once again accompanied us, each loaded with provisions.

At the gap between the peaks the herdsmen turned for home, leaving the beasts of burden in the care of Sergeant Cunningham, who they had come to trust with their animals' welfare.

From the crest of the path between the peaks we looked down into another valley. Unlike Tomasu's home, this valley was dense with trees. More jungle to penetrate. From the jungle rose the chatter of various monkeys. Nor was there any discernible path through it, or at least none that the average man could see. But as you may have surmised by now, Allan Quatermain was no ordinary man.

"Elephants." he said, pointing at the jungle beneath us. "Elephants have pushed their way through. Not many, just a few, each on a solitary journey. But their passage has engineered a road we can follow."

"I thought elephants were pack animals?" I asked, "Why would they wander off alone?"

"To die." responded Quatermain.

"To the same place?" Then I remembered the stories, "The elephants graveyard!"

"That's a myth," snorted Quatermain, "But I think this particular migration is not the work of ordinary pachyderms, rather that it has something to do with your mysterious ivory. If my assumptions are correct, I believe we will find the answers we seek at the end of this elephant road."

As I mentioned neither, Cunningham or myself could see the 'road' he mentioned, and I'm not sure Tomasu could either, but to Quatermain our route was as clear as the Great North Road out of London.

Once we descended to the jungle floor we began to see what Quatermain had seen, a path driven through the trees by the passage of several large animals. As we started along this strange terminal path, I began to feel apprehensive and queried Quatermain as to our chances of encountering an elephant en-route.

"It doesn't look like this road has been used for several months," he explained after examining the pathway in some detail, "but that doesn't mean it won't be used again. But have no concern. We will hear the approach of any elephant long before we see it."

I wasn't exactly comforted by this explanation.

As it turned out it wasn't an elephant that followed us on this stage of our journey, instead it was a small band of chimpanzees. At first we were alerted to their presence by a low murmur of chatter from the tree branches that seemed to stay with us as we made progress. The first night we stopped we caught sight of something moving in the shadows just away from the light thrown by our campfire. The second night the shadow moved closer revealing itself as a large chimpanzee, which Quatermain decided must have been the alpha-male of the band trailing us. On the third night the chimp ventured forward to the edge of our camp and stood watching us with as much curiosity as we watched it. After a while Cunningham threw the remains of a ripe banana he had been eating in the chimp's direction. The ape immediately made a grab for it, and with prize in hand scuttled back to the trees where his return was greeted with howls of approval.

Despite Quatermain's admonishments and caution about encouraging the beasts, Cunningham kept up the practice of feeding the chimp over several nights, each time drawing the animal closer into our camp. We all thought this was great fun, until the one evening where instead of just the one chimp, we found ourselves surrounded by what appeared to be all the adult chimps from the group that had been following us, probably about thirty in number, although I never took an accurate count.

The chimps just stood looking at us.

Not a sound emanated from their lips. They just stared.

Then the chatter started. At first it was the low murmur we had heard from the trees during the daylight hours. But it gradually rose and changed until it matched the howls of approval we had come to associate with the return of the leader with his nightly prize of food.

The food! I think we all realized at the same time what the chimps had come for. Laid out on the ground between us was our planned supper for that evening, while nearby sat our various baskets of provisions, all with the lids open.

"Don't make any sudden moves." the whispered advice came from Quatermain. But it was too late for me. I'd made a dive to grab and close the two baskets closest to me. A foolish move on my part.

I don't know if it was my sudden move, or some sort of signal from the alpha-male, but suddenly the chimps were on us. Clambering over us and around us trying to grab whatever foodstuff they could. The four of us were buried in a mass of excited, uncontrollable, muscle, hair, and teeth.

Perhaps because he regarded him as the leader of our group, the large alpha-male had attached himself to Cunningham and was beating on the soldier's chest with his massive paws while screaming into the poor man's face. As I struggled to remove a couple of smaller chimps from my back, I saw Cunningham react as any soldier might; he reached for his sidearm.

Withdrawing his revolver he aimed it skywards with, I believe, the intention of loosing of a round to scare the chimps away. As his arm went up, the large alpha-male took hold and dragged it downward.

The report of Cunningham's pistol going off echoed around the forest like a preternatural role of thunder. A sound unheard in these environs. A new sound of fury and death. The chimpanzees yowled, this time in a frenzy of panic, rather than anger. All made a hasty retreat back into the treetops.

Quatermain was the first of our party to recover. "We should move, now, while the apes are confused and frightened." He pointed ahead, "Although it is now dusk we should still be able to keep to the trail."

Tomasu moved to step by his side, "The Pale Hunter speaks true. The shock will wear off and they may come back to look for us."

"I think they will more likely return for that." Cunningham's morose voice made us turn and look in his direction. At his feet lay the figure of the alpha-male, the side of its skull blasted away by the shot from Cunningham's sidearm. It was a ghastly and shocking sight. I have seen bodies before, human bodies, more than I dare to think off. Some in bad condition, for a body dragged out of an African river after several days submerged is not a pretty sight, but the body of that poor chimp seemed to provoke a deeper reaction to sudden violent death than any other I'd hereto experienced.

"Dear God!" I exclaimed.

"Shouldn't we bury it?" asked Cunningham, "It seems the decent thing to do."

Tomasu placed a hand on his shoulder, "Neither your god, nor anyone else's holds sway over the ways of the jungle. They will not return for him. They will leave his body to rot and feed the jungle, while they fight among themselves until a new leader of their group emerges. Do not grieve for them."

With reluctance we heeded the Chieftain's advice and left the body behind, and continued on our path. But then Cunningham and I were witness to a most puzzling scene.

We were but a yard or so along the path when a noise behind us made the two of us turn around and look back at the site of the altercation. As we looked something dropped out of the trees. At first glance I thought it was another ape, but this was like no ape I'd seen before. It is true that it moved like an ape, but its movements didn't appear to be naturally those of a simian. Its head and shoulders seemed covered in matted straggly hair rather than fur, while its body seemed almost hairless in comparison. It was however covered in a mix of scratches, scar tissue and caked on grime and mud. As it pawed the area it also sniffed the air. Suddenly it stopped, and perhaps catching our scent, looked in our direction for a second. I gasped, for out the mass of hair on and around the face, I found myself locking gaze with a pair of piercing blue eyes.

The moment passed and this strange creature turned again, and in a single movement swept up the body of the fallen chimp, and bounded back into the treetops.

Dumbfounded at what we had seen, I turned to Cunningham, the first of many questions forming on my lips. But his countenance radiated a look that signaled that he didn't want to talk about the strange apparition. So in communicable silence we turned again back on to our path.

Elephants are fascinating creatures. Both familial in nature, yet seemingly adept at also living a solitary existence. It was about two days after our encounter with the strange blue-eyed hairless ape that we encountered an aged bull elephant on the trail. It was heading in the same direction as us, presumably on its way to die as Quatermain had surmised.

Naturally it was Quatermain who first become aware of the beast's presence ahead. Having announced his finding, he quickened his pace to leave Tomasu, Cunningham, and I trailing as he went ahead to ascertain more about our new traveling companion.

"I believe we have found our guide," Quatermain announced when he rejoined our party a few hours later. "The beast is old and will remain docile if we don't interfere with its journey. If we follow at a discreet distance it will lead us to the destination we seek."

"How can you be so certain of that, old friend?" asked Tomasu.

"You will see when we catch up to it," replied Quatermain somewhat enigmatically, "now come, we have an elephant to catch."

Being a river trader, my experience of elephants has been limited to occasional encounters with families of them standing riverside drinking, and washing themselves. Occasionally one would wade into deeper water, but on the whole I have steered clear of them, and they of me. If truth be told I have harbored a certain curiosity about what it would be like to encounter one close up, but the creature we found ourselves following through the jungle on this particular occasion was nothing like anything I'd seen, or imagined.

I estimated that the beast measured at least fifteen feet from the ground to the ridgeline along its back. You would expect an animal of that size to have an expansive girth, yet this one was almost emaciated. A parchment like grey skin stretched tight over bones. You could see the outline of its ribs and backbone as it moved, the skin flakey and peeling in places. It was almost cadaver like. Bent and scarred legs carried this sorry frame in a slow plodding pace that we could easily match. The large head was held low in an attitude of resignation, and the eyes were milky opaque, making me consider that if it wasn't already blind, it was certainly on the way to being so.

Although now a pathetic looking beast, I surmised that it had once been a formidable creature, a hypothesis supported by my first sight of its most magnificent feature, its tusks. These were the largest and longest tusks I had ever seen, and I'd seen some magnificent specimens brought in by hunters to various river staging posts during my time in Africa. In girth they were about as wide as a man's leg, and tapered out as far as the elephant was tall. To accommodate their length they curved down to almost touch the ground. I'm sure the sheer weight of them was the cause for the beast's head down posture. In fact it must have taken what little strength it still possessed to stop them dragging on the ground.

As we followed it into an open area on the path, it took advantage of the space to swing its head around to take a look at the group of men following it. As those tusks swung into the sunlight, we caught sight of the now familiar irrelevant glitter.

"Holy...." gasped Cunningham. "Golden ivory."

"As I said," confirmed Quatermain, "he will lead us."

We followed Gordon, for that was the name that Cunningham soon bestowed upon our pachyderm guide (I assumed as a reference to General Gordon, recently arrived in Africa), for several days. His passage through the jungle growth was less than subtle as he used the long tusks to pull and

*"These were the largest and longest tusks…"*

rip away anything that had overgrown his ancestral path. I fretted that the noise might draw predators, but Quatermain assured me that the exact opposite was the case; that no animal would get in the way of a mammoth like this one.

The march was relentless for Gordon never seemed to stop. He had no need of sustenance for this was a death march, but we did. A few times a day we would stop for an hour to rest and eat, and once refreshed sprint after the elephant along the path it had driven through the undergrowth. In this way we managed to keep pace with it.

It was after one such stop that I came close to emulating Gordon on a fatal journey.

Normally Sergeant Cunningham would be at the head of our quartet as we sprinted after the animal, his seeming empathy for beasts of all size and disposition driving him forward, yet for some reason on this day he had hung back to discuss something with Tomasu and Quatermain, and not being party to the discussion I headed out on my own. My mind must have been elsewhere, although what occupied it at that point I couldn't say. In short I wasn't looking where I was going and only realized the fact that Gordon had veered off the path as I passed his bulk. I do remember registering the fact that the elephant seemed to have its trunk in the air as if sniffing something, the first time I had seen it raise its head since we started following it.

That particular observation didn't stay with me very long, for with my next step the ground disappeared from beneath me and I fell into blackness.

I probably only fell for a second or two, but it felt like a lifetime.

My rapid descent came to a sudden stop as the leathery trunk of our elephant friend wrapped itself around my waist. Twisting my head around I could see those two enormous tusks above me spanning the hole into which I'd fallen. They represented a possible bridge to freedom but lay tantalizingly just out of reach. I tried calling to the animal trying to encourage him to lift me up and back away from the edge of the precipice. He stayed exactly where he was. There we both stayed, seemingly stuck. As my nerves calmed and the adrenaline rush from the fall subsided I began to gain greater awareness of my surroundings. It was then I noticed the smell. The unmistakable rancid odor of rotting meat. It must have been this that had alerted Gordon and caused him to side step away from this trap, for that was what I now realized the hole to be. From what I could see of the edges they were too even and straight for natural erosion. Whatever this trap was for, it was man-made.

I twisted around in the elephant's trunk, hoping that my movement would not give him cause for alarm resulting in him losing his grip, but the hold stayed firm as I maneuvered myself to examine my surroundings closer. The bottom of the pit was hidden in shadow, but the combination of the rising sun and my eyes adjusting to the gloom beneath me slowly revealed more details.

What I beheld was, to put it simply, a charnel house. The pit was littered with the skeletons and rotting carcasses of several different denizens of the surrounding jungles. All had perished on the series of uneven wooden spikes that lined the floor and the bottom third of the walls. If my descent had been just a few feet lower I would have joined them.

One body above all the others caught my attention. The sight and smell of it causing the bile to rise in my stomach and for me to vomit its contents onto the horror below me. For this particular body wasn't that of any jungle animal, but that of a man, and judging from the remnants of clothing that still clung to the body, that of a civilized man.

The body was too ravaged by time, and the scurrying rodents and insects that feasted on the flesh in the pit, for me to even begin to try and make any attempt to reconstruct in my mind what this man had looked like in life. As I stared at the horrific sight in front of me, I began to realize that I did in fact recognize the remnants of cloth clinging to the cadaver. The impaled corpse lying before me was that of my erstwhile, Germanic benefactor, Karl. Whatever his grand scheme had been to escape the Dark Continent it had ended in agony in this deep, dark, dank pit of death.

And now my own survival appeared to be dependent on the strength and patience of an ailing elephant.

There seemed to be nothing I could do but wait out my fate. Gordon would either grow bored and move back, hopefully pulling me out of the hole, or he would grow tired and drop me to my death below. I resigned myself to destiny, and closed my eyes, trying to relax as I awaited my fate.

I felt something tickle the back of my neck. Still keeping my eyes shut I shrugged it away taking it for some insect or other that had alighted on my back. But there it was again, and again. Why I grew irritated at such a trifle given my predicament I'll never know, but irritated I was, and snapped my eyes open. There hanging in front of me was a pair of well-worn boots.

Boots belonging to none other than Allan Quatermain. I twisted around to once more face upwards, and ended up looking at his grinning countenance. He was dangling in the pit help by a twisted rope of vines that were circled around his chest. In his hand he held a similar vine rope that dangled free; it was obviously this with which he had been trying to attract my attention.

"Sorry to disturb your slumber, Daniel."

My response to such levity was to just stare at him dumfounded. He was grinning, his whole face lit up and his demeanor that of a man half his age. Here he was hanging from a vine over a pit of sharpened stakes, after being lowered between the tusks of an aged elephant, and yet he was clearly enjoying every second of it. At last Allan Quatermain was face to face with peril and was very much in his element. He gestured to the top of the pit and the rope slackened dropping him down a few feet more until we were face to face. "Not to worry" he said in a tone of voice I hadn't heard him use before, one that was both soothing, yet commanding. "The good Sergeant is keeping Gordon calm. He seems to have a natural way with beasts of any size and persuasion."

With that Quatermain leant forward and wrapped the other rope under my arms, tightening it into a loop. He then did something I'll never forget. He swung himself around in that pit of death until he had lined himself up with the end of the elephant's trunk. Once in position he gently blew into the nostrils at the end of the extended proboscis, which promptly uncurled from around my waist.

I dropped like a stone, heading for the spikes below. My downward motion being bought to a sudden and violent halt by the vine rope looped under my arms. My feet just a few inches above the top of the tallest deadly spikes. If Quatermain had misjudged the length I would have been as dead as Karl. As it was the two of use now hung in the pit rocking backwards and forwards like the pendulum of a broken clock. I looked at Quatermain, and in a less than gracious voice enquired, "Now what?"

"Now, my dear River Rat, we ascend." And with that he gave a tug on his rope.

Nothing happened.

He tugged again.

Still nothing.

We looked at each other. Quatermain's countenance shifted from the boyish grin to one of concern. He went from adventurer to hunter in the blink of an eye. But before we could exchange a single syllable I was suddenly hauled upward with a speed that almost matched my earlier fall. I burst into the sunlight above the hole, and before I could gain my footing was dragged bodily across the pathway to end up with my back slamming against a tree, around which I noticed our vine ropes were looped into a carved slot around the circumference. Quatermain and my friends had obviously being using the trunk and vines as a crude makeshift rope and pulley system.

Smart thinking.

I turned to congratulate Cunningham and Tomasu, who I assumed would be on the end of the rope. Instead I found myself staring at the ugliest native brute I think I have ever seen.

The man I was looking at was at least as tall as Tomasu, but in contrast to our friend's athletic frame this native seemed to be as wide as he was tall. His bloated rotund figure must have carried at least twenty-five stone if not more. But the striking thing was that when he moved it didn't shudder the way you would expect excess amounts of blubber to, this massive body was all toned muscle. Around his equally massive waist he wore a girdle of twisted vine and leaves from which hung a collection of shrunken heads, similar to the one worn by Tomasu on ceremonial occasions. However this one did not appear to be an old family heirloom. It was a functional display of recent victims, a symbol of power and authority over his fellow man. Tucked into this horrific belt was a large machete style knife with a handle fashioned from what I was beginning to easily identify as golden ivory. His torso, arms and legs were covered with a combination of tattooed patterns and devices, while the skin beneath these decorations was a mix of scars from numerous wounds inflicted by both man made weapons and various jungle beasts. But the most horrific aspect to the Brute, for that was what I had christened him in my mind, was his face, or what was left of it. As I sat back against the tree he leaned close in to my face to sneer at me. It looked like he had lost half of his face to some savage wild beast, maybe a lion or similar. The left cheek and lower jaw were gone, now only covered by stretched parchment like skin. The left eye was as clouded as the ones of our elephant friend, while the area around the socket and surrounding forehead and nose tissue was crisscrossed with infected scar tissue, inflicted by the teeth of whatever had caused the damage I supposed.

He lifted his left hand towards me and I noticed that it too had been damaged as three fingers were missing with only thumb and forefinger remaining. No matter the lack of digits, I can attest that the hand could still deliver a solid blow as he used it to backhand me across the cheek while directing a steam of foul smelling spittle on to my face.

The blow spun my head around so I ended up staring off to the path at the side of the pit, what I saw made my heart sink even further.

A group of around a dozen natives, all decorated similarly to, but smaller in stature than, my gargantuan assailant were surrounding Gordon goading him to move by jabbing at his sides and the back of his legs with spear points. From the number of fresh cuts I could see I surmised that this cruel treatment had been going on for some time, but the beast was refusing to move. Across the back of the elephant I spotted the bound figures of Tomasu and Cunningham, neither of which appeared to be moving. Despite the frequency with which I take his name in vain, I don't consider myself a man of God, but even so at that moment I silently prayed that they were unconscious and not dead.

It seemed that any hope of salvation now lay with Quatermain.

As if he read my thoughts the Brute reached for the other vine wrapped around the tree, the one on which Quatermain had been lowered to my rescue, and began to pull. The vine rope came up quickly and easily. Too easily.

When it cleared the pit's threshold it was clear that Allan Quatermain was no longer attached.

The Brute strode over to the edge of the pit, looked into it, and then started to laugh, a cruel sound that made me shiver. There could only be one conclusion from witnessing this tableau; Quatermain now lay alongside Karl on the deadly spikes below.

Still chuckling to himself the Brute returned to stand in front of me, and seeing my look of despair started to laugh even louder. He raised his hand again, and this time the blow was sufficient to render me oblivious to my surroundings and fate.

When I awoke it was to find myself staring into the smiling face of Sergeant Cunningham.

"Thank God, I was beginning to wonder if you would ever wake up, River Rat."

Shaking my head to clear my mind, I uttered that most unforgivable of clichés, "Where are we?" I asked.

"In a cave." Responded my companion, thankfully not pointing out that if I'd bothered to take a few seconds to look around before speaking that I could have ascertained that fact for myself. "That's all we know, although it must be close to a village as they bring us fresh food once a day."

"How long?"

"You've been out two days longer than I, Tomasu says he was awake for a day prior to that. How many days since we left the area of that accursed pit, we have no idea."

The mention of the pit bought one word to my lips, "Quatermain?"

Cunningham just shook his head in silent grief.

Looking around I couldn't see our other companion, "Where's Tomasu?"

Cunningham pointed towards the darkness at the rear of the cave. "Exploring, although I told him he's wasting his time. I can't believe they would have cut our bonds and thrown us in here if there was any possibility of escape."

"Why have they kept us alive?"

"Tomasu says the time isn't right."

"Right for what?"

"The ceremony"

My thoughts went to the hideous girdle of shrunken heads, added in the fact that our captives were keeping us fed, and came to one conclusion. A single word passed my lips as the truth of our fate dawned. "Oh."

Cunningham nodded mouthing a simple "Yes," in acknowledgement of my moment of realization.

Before I had time to contemplate our fate any further, Tomasu appeared from the gloom at the back of the cave. "Good to see you awake, Daniel," he greeted me. "And from the ashen look on your face would I be safe in assuming that the Sergeant has shared our speculation as to the grisly end our hosts have planned for us."

"He didn't go into details," I responded, "but basically, yes."

"Any luck?" broke in Cunningham.

"Unfortunately, as I suspected, there is no egress at the rear of this cave, however there is small opening which is the source of the breeze we can feel flowing through here."

"How wide is it?" I asked, "I'm smaller than either of you."

"Sorry to say it is too narrow even for a river rat," Tomasu shrugged, "at its widest I'd say it's no more than the girth of my arm. I tried bellowing several times up the pipe to see if I could attract the attention of anyone who might help us, but I'm afraid the only audience I drew consisted of several chimpanzees. Although they seemed to be interested in the sounds emanating from the hole in the ground, even chattering in response, I doubt we will be able to count on them for any aid."

"We're doomed then." Cunningham's words were more a statement than a question.

We were left to consider our fate for two more days. During those forty-eight hours we talked through various escape scenarios, deeming each impractical and doomed to failure. The thought did pass amongst us that it might be preferable to be killed in battle trying to obtain our freedom; but Tomasu was of the opinion that our captives would be more likely to wound than kill, as they liked their meat fresh, we would therefore spend our last hours in pain. Better he argued to stay fit and alert so we could help each other. So it was we spent the last few hours in that cave concocting schemes to help each other pass quickly once the final torture started.

They came for us at dawn. A procession lead by a small wizened old man whose belt, in contrast to the other cannibals (for that is how we now considered our captives) was not covered with shrunken human heads, but decorated with the skulls of various small monkeys. This I assumed was the tribe's priest or similar. Despite his diminutive size all the warriors seemed a little afraid of him and obeyed his directions without question. We were placed in line in the procession with three warriors lined up between each of us preventing any chance of us communicating with, our aiding, each other. Thus effectively isolated we were marched down from the hillside cave into the village below.

Like many other native collectives I had seen, the cannibals' village was of a circular design, around the perimeter was a rough palisade constructed of logs hacked from the surrounding jungle to stop any encroaching beasts. There was just one opening, the one through which we were currently passing. Just inside the fence was an area of open ground which any intruder, man or beast, would have to pass unprotected before reaching the inner circle of huts. Although open, this inner area did show signs of industry such as millstones, forges, and most sickeningly, an obviously well used and stained butcher's block. The circle of huts was two rows deep, the outer huts being smaller, with the larger huts of the more important tribal members being inside and ranged around a central plaza.

It was into this central common area that we were now marched and the sight that meet our eyes made our imagined fate suddenly come into harsh focus. It was no longer a theoretical exercise, now I knew that we were going to die.

Three thick poles, each about six feet in height, had been placed upright a yard or more apart. Stacked near each pole was dry brushwood, and laid out on a plank by each was a series of crude looking cutting instruments.

Waiting for our arrival in the center of the village was the giant Brute we had first encountered at the pit. Across his ugly deformed face was something that approximated a grin. In his hand he held a large machete.

The Brute motioned in my direction with the machete and uttered some guttural command that rested in a cheer from the watching villagers ranged around the edge of the plaza. Two of the three warriors behind me grabbed my arms while the third propelled me forward towards the cannibal chief. No matter how I felt about my impending doom, I was determined no to show any fear in front of the Brute. He growled in my face, trying to elicit some response, but I remained passive and stoically silent. After a minute or so, the Brute swung his machete down, cutting through the remnants of clothing I still wore, which I'll admit was not in too great a shape following our various adventures. I now stood naked and pale before him. The sight of my pale white skin elicited a smirk from him; he then used the point of his blade to point again at my paleness, shouting something to his audience that resulted in howls of appreciative laughter. It was then he spotted the pouch still hanging around my neck, deftly hefting the large blade he cut through the cord, grabbing the falling pouch and then throwing it in the direction of the shrunken priest.

Robbed of all my worldly possessions, and stripped naked as the day I was born, I was marched to the central pole, where using vine ropes I was lashed tight enough to stop the circulation in my arms and legs. Here I was left to contemplate my fate as the Brute's attention turned to my companions.

Cunningham's treatment was similar to mine, and in short order the Sergeant was trussed to the stake to my right. As I looked a across at him he had his head raised skyward, his eyes shut, and was murmuring something. Perhaps a prayer or two. I hadn't taken him for a religious man, but it was probably a reasonable choice when it came to how to spend our last few minutes.

Tomasu's reception at the hands of the Brute was very different. The cannibal used the blade of the machete to slowly inflict various cuts across his rival chieftain's torso, arms and legs. The shouts from the crowd were closer to jeers of derision than the humor that had accompanied our white skins.

Once Tomasu's garments and adornments had been removed, this time with wide careless sweeps of the blade that inflicted more damage to his body, he was paraded around the circle in humiliation. On his return the center, the brute produced a smaller knife, with which he sliced off a chunk of flesh from Tomasu's cheek, which he then proceeded to eat raw.

The sight of this atrocity made me scream out in a combination of revulsion and terror, but through all the torture, humiliation, and even the mutilation, Tomasu remained silent. For those who chose to look, with every indignity, the hatred grew in his eyes.

Tomasu was eventually tied to the post on my left, and the brush wood was stacked around our feet.

Once the preparations were complete, the Brute called out a command. But strangely no one answered or moved. A murmur arose in the crowd and all eyes, including those of the Brute, turned to look towards one particular hut. I realized that this was the direction I'd seen the priest run off to after he'd caught my pouch. I surmised that this hut must have been his, and the ceremony was now waiting on his blessing to proceed. Did even cannibals feel the need for grace before they feasted? Why such an absurd notion should pass through my mind at such a moment, I had no idea.

No one appeared.

The Brute called again. Still no sign of the priest.

The Brute roared again.

Nothing.

The cannibal chief grunted in anger and strode across the plaza, screaming what I assumed to be the priest's name, a sound something like Z'ula. His entrance to the hut was followed by a few seconds silence, before the whole village heard him erupt into a berserker fury. The screams of rage mixed with crashes of pottery. I guessed that Z'ula, if that was his name, had deserted his post.

Eventually the chief emerged from the hut brandishing a carved log atop which flickered a clump of flaming oil soaked cloth. With a snarl he walked up to my stake and started to lower the flame towards the tinder like brushwood. My end was at hand.

I had decided to meet my fate with my eyes open. I'll be forever glad that I did, for what I witnessed next will stay with me forever.

As the giant cannibal Brute bent to seal my doom, an equally large figure burst upon the scene at great speed hitting the chief with an almighty impact that threw the behemoth to the ground. Arms and legs flailed in what had clearly become a death struggle. Amazingly none of the watching cannibal warriors made a move to aid their chief. I guessed that to offer any assistance would have dishonored him. So they, like us, watched on in silence.

The two giants continued to struggle, blows were exchanged, and then the morning sun caught the sudden flash of a blade. A battle royal had developed over the machete as the two combatants rolled around the plaza, kicking up clouds of dust obscuring the details of their struggle.

I was so focused on the epic battle that it took me a few seconds to realize that my bounds had been severed. The sudden tingling in my restored circulation providing notice that the restriction had been lifted. I glanced behind me to see a sight that I thought I'd never see again.

A grinning Allan Quatermain.

A man I thought dead.

Before I could question this marvelous resurrection he simply nodded and moved on to slice the bonds holding our companions.

As I vigorously shock my arms in order to restore the circulation as quickly as possible I returned my attention to the dueling giants in front of me. The two bodies continued to roll around in the dust, seemingly locked in a deadly impasse, Neither man seeming to be gaining an advantage. And just as suddenly as the fight had started, it stopped.

The two lay still on the floor. A trickle of blood seeping from the space between their bodies.

At the sight, two of the cannibal warriors broke from the watching circle and raced to the aid of their chief. They struggled to pull the body of the strange attacker off the Brute, but as they did do they rolled him over on to his back, giving me a clear look at his features for the first time. The single arm, and the pock marked, spider scarred face confirmed my growing suspicion: our improbable savior was the Frenchman.

Now he lay comatose on his back in a village full of cannibals, a chest wound seeping blood. His opponent, the chieftain, seemed to be in a worse state. He was dead. From the marks of the wounds I surmised that the machete blade had been between the two.

At the sight of their chief's fate, the two warriors began a piercing, wailing cry. A lament soon taken up by the rest of the villagers.

Suddenly the lament changed to a blood-curdling scream and about a dozen warriors rushed forward from the crowd, seemingly bent on revenge for their chief's fate. And we were their targets.

Standing there, naked, and with numb limbs, and no weapons to hand, we were once again at the mercy of fate, for there was nothing we could do to defend ourselves.

Once again, fate's agent turned out to be named Quatermain.

The elephant hunter stepped out from behind the stakes, where he had just finished freeing Tomasu and placed himself between the three of us and the charging warriors. As he strode forward the years seem to fall away from Quatermain's posture, despite his claims to the contrary, he

*"The two combatants rolled around the plaza..."*

was clearly a man who thrived in action. Somewhere he had obtained a whip, which he now wielded with devastating effect.

There was no intention of taking up a defensive posture, swinging and cracking the whip above his head, Quatermain strode out to meet the warriors head on. The whip caught the lead warrior in the side of the face, leaving a deep gash in his cheek, and driving him to the ground in shock and pain. Not stopping to survey his handiwork, Quatermain continued to swing the whip in a continuous arc, inflicting similar damage on two more warriors. Wary of the cracking weapon the other warriors fanned out to encircle him, but Quatermain quickly circled with them, making sure not to keep his back exposed to any single warrior for more than a few seconds.

At some unseen signal warriors suddenly moved in from either side. A couple more felt the sting of Quatermain's whip, but the strength in numbers proved to be an advantage and they got close enough that the arcing whip became less of a threat. Sensing his opponents' change in tactics, the elephant hunter adapted. Grabbing the tail of the whip he now used it as a noose, catching one of the warriors around the neck, drawing him in close to use as a human shield. But these savages have no sense of comradeship or respect for their fellows. The shield proved to be useless as the captured warrior was quickly stabbed by his fellows' spears. A necessary sacrifice to get to the enemy behind.

Realizing the futility of his strategy, Quatermain abandoned the chokehold and the whip and went on the attack, dodging between thrusting spears he dove at the nearest warrior, fists flying. The upper cut that connected with the warriors jaw was as good as any you would see from a professional pugilist. The cannibal was laid low in an instant. It was now one against seven, but the shock of Quatermain's bold moves was wearing off, and the warriors started to co-ordinate their efforts.

The seemingly ageless elephant hunter wasn't going to go down without a fight. He dove towards the largest of the remaining cannibals in a perfect rugby tackle, bringing his man down. Now with no weapons of his own to hand, Quatermain struggled with the downed warrior for control of his spear. As the two fought the remaining half dozen advanced on them. All I could contribute was to shout a warning to Quatermain about the group advancing on his exposed back.

Just as the cannibals reached the struggling pair, Quatermain managed to flip himself and his opponent over so that he now lay with his back on the ground and the warrior on top of him, the disputed spear pointing upwards where the first of the arriving warriors impaled himself on it, leaving Quatermain now pinned beneath two of the tribesmen, one dead and one still very much alive and struggling.

The other five continued to move towards the struggle, when suddenly a large figure appeared behind them. It was the Frenchman. He grabbed the rearward cannibal around the neck with his one good arm and gave a quick sharp twist and with the sickening sound of his neck snapping the man slumped to the floor.

Sensing the new danger behind them, the remaining four turned to face the gigantic Frenchman, spears ready to be thrown.

"STOP!"

The cry, surprisingly in English, rang out across the plaza.

Even if all the combatants didn't understand the word, the tone conveyed the meaning. Everyone paused to look at the source. It was Tomasu, and stood beside him was the shrunken figure of the village priest, Z'ula

Z'ula shouted something in his own tongue, and the surviving warriors stepped back, dropping their weapons. The one struggling with Quatermain, ceased his fight and, after standing up, reached a hand down to help his former adversary upright.

Quatermain, Cunningham and I, while still keeping a watchful eye on the cannibals, walked over to where Tomasu and the priest were standing. "Can you understand their language?"

Cunningham asked Tomasu.

"It shares a common ancestry with my own native language. I can interpret enough to get a basic understanding." he responded.

"So what did he say that caused them to take us off the menu?" Cunningham asked.

Tomasu let out a slight laugh as he replied, "You may not believe this, but if I understood him correctly he told them that we were not to be harmed as we were the emissaries of the naked white goddess."

"The what?" the three of us chorused.

"The naked white goddess."

"What naked white goddess?" I responded in some bemusement.

"Yours, Daniel."

"Mine?"

Tomasu bent down to whisper something to the priest beside him. Z'ula nodded and with great care and dignity reached into my pouch, which he now wore on his belt rope, and produced the faded Parisian postcard that had been among the artifacts Karl had given me. As he held it up a murmur spread around the village plaza.

Somebody had some explaining to do.

So it was that we found ourselves seated and feted as honored guests in the hut of the priest, a man who not an hour previously had been leading the ceremony intended to prepare us to be eaten by his fellow villagers.

Western style clothes had been found for myself and Cunningham, where these had been sourced from I dare not think too hard on. Tomasu's tribal regalia had been returned, as had our weapons, including Quatermain's whip. A magnanimous gesture of trust on Z'ula's part given the circumstances.

We were sat in a circle around what looked to be a small altar in the center of the priest's hut, while he, through a mixture of hand gestures and rough translations via Tomasu told us his story.

To start the lecture he pulled back a cloth that had been covering something on the altar, exposing a small statuette of maybe six inches in height. It was a crude rendition of a naked woman, typical of many of the fertility symbols found in central Africa, but this one appeared to have been fired from a light clay that gave it the appearance of having white skin color. It also glittered with the same golden sheen the ivory had.

Z'ula explained that the icon had been with the tribe for many generations, its origins lost to time. When they first encountered white men they believed them to be emissaries of the goddess and welcomed them into the village, even sharing the secret of the elephants, at this phrase we all exchanged quick glances. But they were betrayed, and robbed. Soon they refused to trust any white man.

Until recently, when a white man had stumbled into their village, carrying with him tokens of the naked white goddess. It only took a few questions on our part to confirm that this had been my Germanic benefactor. After being shown the secret of the elephants he had declared that he would one day return with other white men such as he to protect the secret.

None of us could bring ourselves to tell the priest that Karl had been no different from the other white men. It was now apparent that his sure fire scheme to get out of Africa involved harvesting as much golden ivory as he could. I wondered, were we any different?

"What about the elephants?" the inevitable question had been asked. The questioner was Quatermain.

Man. Of all the creatures that inhabit the African jungle, I believe the one that I understand the least is my own species. Like the other denizens of the wild we live to survive through the hunting of food, as well as being driven by the need for shelter and procreation. But on top of this we layer so much else that we mask our true natures, even from each other. Even from those we consider companions and friends.

The answer to Quatermain's question about the elephants started about two miles outside the village with signs of a trail. A trail, which to Quatermain's experienced eye, showed signs of being well used by the creatures. A continuation of the pachyderm road on which we had encountered Gordon.

Z'ula said little as he and Quatermain lead our strange expedition onwards. The two occasionally pointing out signs that no one else could read, or even necessarily see, to confirm we were on the right trail.

Our party consisted of our two leads, Tomasu, Cunningham, the Frenchman, followed by half a dozen warriors, including the one with whom Quatermain had been locked in the death struggle the day before, and myself.

It was about six hours into our journey, when Tomasu waved us all to a halt. He pointed up at the tree canopy. At first I couldn't see what had caught his attention, but the then I spotted it; a chimpanzee. Personally I didn't see why this should merit our attention; the small apes were common enough. Tomasu started to slowly circle in place pointing at different areas of the foliage above us. Each place he pointed I spotted a different chimpanzee. More and more of them. It was like a regiment of simians was observing us.

The tall warrior, Quatermain's former nemesis, panicked. His spear flew upwards. There was a high pitched shriek, followed by a thud as a chimp fell to the ground.

"What did you do that for?" Cunningham screamed at the warrior before crashing off the path into the surrounding jungle in search of the unfortunate victim. I believe Cunningham still harbored feelings of guilt over his accidental slaying of the chimp earlier in our adventure. Whatever his reasons for hunting for the body we will never know.

Shortly after his departure a terrible noise rose through the jungle. A combination of scream and yodel. An inhuman sound, but not one I could match to the throat of any known animal. It seemed to come from the same direction in which Cunningham had set off.

Quatermain, as he often did, reacted first, beckoning Z'ula, Tomasu and a handful of warriors to stay on the path, while indicating that the Frenchman, myself and the tall warrior should follow him.

Cunningham's passage through the undergrowth had not been a subtle one; his path was easy to follow.

We came across him in a small clearing. He sat with his back to a tree. The body of the fallen chimp was in his arms, as if comforting a swaddling babe. He looked in peaceful repose. But the vine rope around his neck told a different story.

It wrapped around and cut deep into his neck, raising a series of hellish looking purple and red welts. His tongue protruded in a cruel imitation of a comedic response often employed by young boys. At the rear of the noose we could see the vine rope extend upward where it was looped and tied around a high branch. We just stood and stared at the fate of our companion.

After several moments of silence, Quatermain walked forward and examined the body. It looks like he had the noose dropped over his head from above and was then hauled upwards. He never let go of the chimp."

"But how?" I stammered, "No animal uses ropes like that. Only men."

"Agreed." said a somber Quatermain, "but what sort of man."

The tall warrior mumbled something that we could not understand, but his fear was clear. He turned and fled back to join the rest of the party.

Without the tools to bury our companion, we reluctantly decided to leave him to the animals he had clearly loved, and had died trying to protect in his own way.

It was with heavy hearts that the three of us returned to the pathway, to find the rest of the party in disarray. The tall warrior was in an animated argument with the priest, while the other cannibals kept muttering a word over and over again.

"What are they saying, Tomasu?" asked Quatermain.

"Forgive me Pale Hunter," responded Tomasu, "but I do not know. It is a word new to me. It appears to be a name. But whatever it is, it appears to be a name of great power and fear."

At this point Z'ula broke off from his argument with a dramatic wave of the arms, and headed in our direction. He conversed with Tomasu for a while before returning to his argument.

Tomasu recounted the conversation as best he could. "It seems the name is a word used by the tribe to describe something out here in the jungle, it describes something more than ape, but less than man. A strange animal that protects the jungle. They have never seen it, but they say that strange cry we heard is its killing call. They say it was responsible for the death of the Sergeant."

I thought back to the creature Cunningham and I had seen previously, wondering if this was the mysterious ape they were talking about, but decided to keep my own council. I have no idea why, but it seemed to me that the best thing for everyone would be to keep it a secret. And so I did until this very day.

"The warriors are arguing that they should return to the village for they have angered the protector of the jungle. But the priest says they have an obligation to fulfill, that they must lead the emissaries to the place of the elephants." Tomasu rounded off his narrative.

There was now little we could do but sit and wait the outcome of the argument between a bunch of cannibal warriors and their diminutive priest.

The argument lasted to sundown and beyond. Even after we had set a fire and made camp for the night the unintelligible debate raged. The exchange of native voices soon becoming a monotonous background noise as I drifted off to sleep, with memories of my military friend fresh in my mind.

When I awoke the following morning it seemed that the debate had been settled in the priest's favor as he and the tall warrior were in the midst of sharing a repast of the meat of some small animal, which I noticed they were consuming raw, while the other warriors were positioned equidistant around our camp apparently guarding us from whatever threats might emerge from the jungle.

Once rested and fed we resumed our trek along the elephant path. The next two days walking passed without further incident, although our escort remained on edge, and we all jumped at every chatter of an ape that we heard. We all felt that our every move was being watched, and we had no intention of attracting any further wrath from whatever it was out there, man or beast, or some strange unknown combination of the two.

About midway through the third day the path came to an abrupt end and we found ourselves standing on the edge of a small grotto at the foot of a cliff face.

At the front of the party Z'ula spun around threw his arms wide as if to encompass the scene behind him. With a proud smile he spoke.

We didn't need a translator, for it was apparent to all that we were looking at the elephants' secret.

We had arrived at the culmination of our quest begun many weeks before in the dusty dockside offices of Union & Empire Exports Ltd.

The first thing I noticed about the grotto was the ground, or more specifically the dirt. I have no idea what set of geological parameters it would need to produce such sediment, and I'm sure that this small patch was probably a result of a unique set of circumstances. The ground was of a chalky, almost white, hue and throughout it was flecked with those now so familiar speckles of gold. With the midday sun on it the whole floor of the grotto seemed to shimmer and sparkle. It was obvious were the material for the villager's white goddess had originated.

At the far end of the grotto at the base of the cliff was a waterfall and pool. The pool was full of elephants, both young and old. At first sight it appeared that they were just basking in the water as a way to gain relief from the noon sun, but a closer look one could see them exhibiting a most singular behavior. The younger ones had their tusks buried in the mud banks around the periphery of the pool.

"So that's how it's done." whispered the Frenchman stood alongside me.

"The gold flecks must impregnate the tusks as the mud dries off." I nodded.

"I've never seen anything like it," the last voice was Quatermain's. "Look, there's a familiar face."

We followed his gaze. Sure enough there in the middle of the pool was the old elephant, Gordon.

As if hearing the sound of our voices, the aged pachyderm swung his head in our direction. Given his last encounter with men and the cannibals in particular, it wasn't surprising that his reaction wasn't a friendly one. He raised his trunk bellowing a warning to the other elephants. There followed something close to a stampede as they left the pool en masse and followed Gordon through the waterfall.

"There must be an archway behind there!" Tomasu's voice rang out clear. "Quick, let's follow."

"Give them time to settle," cautioned Quatermain, "we don't want to spook them any further."

"Nonsense," Tomasu's response was almost a challenge. "The Pale Hunter knows what's behind there, he just wants to keep the rest of us away."

"What are you talking about?" I asked.

"An elephants' graveyard!" Tomasu sounded almost as if he was salivating now, "Mounds of golden ivory. Ours just for the taking." and with that he headed off at a run following the path the elephants had taken through the waterfall.

We had little choice but to follow a man we considered a friend, a man who had helped us out in time of tragedy and need. It appeared that now he was a man possessed, the one in need, and was heading for a potential tragedy of his own making.

Ignoring the soaking we rushed through the cascading water at the bottom of the cliff and burst through into a large cavern. Tomasu had been right. The cavern was stacked with the bones, and decaying bodies of generations of elephants. Golden ivory tusks lay everywhere. And standing between the mound and us was the parade of elephants guarding the last resting place of their antecedents. Immediately in front of the agitated elephants paced the crazed figure of Tomasu. Seized by a gold lust I never expected. The man was ranting, "The arrow was proof. This is my tribe's heritage. We will drive these pretenders away. We were the original keepers and the guardians of the golden ivory."

"Tomasu!" Quatermain called out to him, "Old friend, step back and try to calm down."

"You can't fool me, Pale Hunter," called the deranged chieftain, "you want this for yourself, but it shall not be."

Quatermain kept the exchange going as he crept close and closer to where Tomasu stood in his rage. When he felt he was in range Quatermain lunged forward hoping to restrain his friend.

Tomasu caught the movement out of the corner of his eye. He dashed forward, straight into the line of panicked elephants. Numerous massive feet rose and fell around him as he tried to work his way to the golden reward beyond. It didn't take long for the inevitable to happen. In some ways it seemed fitting that old Gordon should prove to be the final guardian. His massive foot caught Tomasu on the side of the head, and we watched helpless as a man we thought we knew met his fate while dreaming of avarice and greed beyond our imaginings. Tomasu fell and before we could move to aid him his body disappeared under a pummeling of elephant feet.

It was several minutes before the herd calmed down. Once they had stilled, Quatermain quietly approached, using all his skills and knowledge of the beasts to appear as non-threatening as possible. He had identified Gordon as the lead male. Once alongside, he calmly led the old elephant back out through the waterfall to the grotto beyond. The rest of the beasts followed.

With the elephants clear, the Frenchman and I cautiously moved forward into the pile of bones and ivory. The stink from the newer decomposing elephant corpses was overwhelming. How anyone could consider this charnel house to be a treasure trove was beyond me.

"What do we do about the gold?" asked the Frenchman.

"I don't know." I responded.

"We leave it." the new voice was Quatermain's. "This is a sacred place for the elephants and for these people." and with that he nodded his head in the direction of Z'ula and his warriors.

"But wasn't the gold the reason we set out on this journey?" I asked.

"You wanted to discover the secret of the golden ivory and the meaning of the tokens left with you. I was hired to find a rumored elephants' graveyard. We have both completed our missions I would say." Quatermain smiled, "and no-one instructed us what to do beyond that brief, so I suggest we leave things as they are. It will be our secret, and theirs. And what of your mission?" Quatermain looked at the Frenchman.

"Mine was a simple task," he smiled, "all I had to do was kill Allan Quatermain. I never asked why, and those who hired me are no more. A debt has been paid."

*On that enigmatic note the old man stopped, His tale at last complete he slumped back in his chair. The effort of sharing this fantastic story had drained him beyond exhaustion.*

*As I wondered what to do next a shadow fell across the old man in the chair and I looked up to see a large pocked faced man with one arm. The large man looked down at the old man with a mix of companionship and concern. He then shifted his gaze to me and spoke in a distinct French accent. "Told you his story, did he?"*

*"Yes," I answered, "but why did he seem so intent on telling it to me of all people?"*

*"Your name."*

*"I never told him my name."*

*"He heard someone call you Sergeant Porter."*

*"What of it?"*

*"He told you of the Professor in Baltimore that inspired his love of Africa?"*

*"He mentioned it."*

*"That Professor and you share a nom-de-familie. Word had reached*

*Daniel that his mentor, and his daughter, had many years later reached Africa's shores and had their own encounter with a mysterious blue-eyed hairless ape; a so-called protector of the jungle. Daniel always hoped that they'd meet again so they could compare adventures, it was not to be. You are the first Porter he has encountered in decades."*

*"I'm flattered, but I don't know of this Professor, nor of any relatives in America come to that."*

*The Frenchman looked down at the old man who had slipped into a quiet slumber in the armchair. "That doesn't matter to him. He needed to tell the tale, and now it's been told."*

*"Before you go, I have a question: what of Quatermain?"*

*"There are many more tales of the elephant hunter left to be shared, but I will tell you this," said the Frenchman, "he taught me that you can be a great hunter without being a killer." As he finished talking he dropped a small leather pouch into my lap. "Here, my friend would want you to have this."*

*With that the large Frenchman scooped his dozing friend up under his one good arm, and as if lifting a child, hefted him up to rest against his shoulder. "Thank you for listening."*

*And the pouch? Inside was a bent and faded postcard, along with what appeared to be the tip of an ivory tusk. I pulled the tip out, and held it up in the ray of sunlight streaming through the hotel lobby window. Rotating it between thumb and forefinger I examined it from every angle. Nothing. Not a hint or glimmer of gold.*

*And so these two strangers, and their strange tale, disappeared from my life. I captured as much as I could in this transcript hoping that I might do my part in ensuring some degree of posterity.*

Sgt. Norman Porter
3rd Battalion, Manchester Regiment
Alexandria
June, 1916.

### THE END

# ABOUT ELEPHANTS

I guess I should thank my grandmother.

She lived with us for a short while when I must have been around seven years old. One of my fondest memories of that time was spending rainy Sunday afternoons watching old movies on the TV with her. She had a great appreciation of classic cinema, but she also enjoyed a good adventure yarn. You'd find us watching a Tarzan flick starring Johnny Weismuller as often as a David O Selznick produced epic like *Gone With The Wind*.

It was on such an afternoon that I first encountered Allan Quatermain. It was a showing of the 1950 version of *Kings Solomon's Mines* starring one of my grandmother's favorite actors, Stewart Granger. I was entranced. Not so much by the story as by the idea of an adventure hero who shared my name (it was only later that I discovered he spelt it differently.) The only other hero named Alan I knew at that point was Alan Tracy from Gerry Anderson's seminal SF/adventure TV show, *Thunderbirds*; but he was a puppet. Quatermain was real. Or at least he seemed it to me.

Over the years, while never rising to the heights of my other fictional heroes like Bond, Allan Quartermain stayed with me. While at high school I set out to track down and read the original Haggard stories, a feat achieved over a couple of years thanks to numerous visits to the local library. Whenever a Quatermain movie was on TV I tried to make sure I watched it. Even after my grandmother had moved on to her own apartment I would still try and head on over to share a Sunday afternoon movie watching with her.

So when the opportunity to add to the legacy of Quatermain arose, I just had to contribute.

It was thinking about those movie afternoons that gave me my initial idea for the story. Quatermain and Tarzan together. Why not? Would it be possible?

Philip Jose Farmer's Wold Newton theory that all the literary heroes are connected suggested that the two characters might even be related. Why not have Quatermain head out on a quest to find a long lost relative who just happened to be a certain jungle lord? I could pitch the elephant hunter against the protector of elephants. - Perfect.

One of the guidelines for this series of new Quatermain adventures would be that they would be set before the events in *King Solomon's Mines*.

On a business trip to San Diego I reread both that book, and *Tarzan of the Apes*. Halfway through Tarzan I realized my story idea wouldn't work. The dates didn't line up. Tarzan's first encounter with a white man happened after the events of *King Solomn's Mines*. So he and Quatermain couldn't meet. But there was no reason that the presence of a younger wild ape-man couldn't be felt throughout Quatermain's jungle adventure.

But what sort of adventure should it be? A classic quest? Of course. Something involving elephants? Naturally.

To try and get my head into period I decided to watch a bunch of different adventure movies set in colonial Africa. After watching Bogart in *The African Queen* I had my opening part of the quest, and my protagonist narrator.

From there it didn't take me long to put together my list of character types I wanted on the quest. However I was having a problem naming them. Nothing I tried seemed to fit their characterizations.

It was another business trip that solved that problem, (I travel a lot with the day job). Sitting in a hotel bar I was enjoying a drink and a meal while doing some research reading for another project when I glanced up at the TV behind the bar. It was showing some big poker game from a glitzy hotel in Las Vegas, and there on screen was the perfect name for my riverboat captain. Out came the notebook, and my reading abandoned, I watched the poker tournament for the next half hour, not studying the turn of the cards, but the turn of the names on screen. By the time I walked out of that bar I had all the names for my cast of characters.

I was ready to set them off on their adventure.

And what an adventure it turned out to be. While I had an initial plot worked out, this final version of the story bears only a passing resemblance to it. As much as Quatermain and his companions didn't know what awaited them around each river bend or jungle path, I found that the story took me places I'd never expected. Characters did things I'd not plotted, with the fate of some decided only as I was typing the words that described it.

*Golden Ivory* turned out to be a grand adventure.

It also sparked ideas for even more Allan Quatermain stories. Stories that I hope to tell at some point in the future.

It's over twenty years since my grandmother passed, and even longer since we shared a movie afternoon, but I'd like to think that she'd have enjoyed this story.

Gran, this one's for you.

**ALAN J. PORTER** - has been writing about the worlds of various pop-culture icons for well over a decade, with non-fiction books on Batman, The Beatles, Star Trek and James Bond. He has also contributed essays to several other books, as well as written numerous magazine articles.

In the world of comics he is perhaps best known as the writer of the Disney*Pixar CARS comic book series from BOOM! Studios, and he still writes the occasional CARS story for Disney Publishing. He has also had work published by Tokyopop and Marvel and is currently writing a new series called *Forgotten City*, as well as pitching various ideas to any comics publisher that will listen.

As well as various short-stories for Airship27, he is currently working on *The James Bond Lexicon* to be published by Hasslein Books in late 2013 or early 2014.

# TEMPLE OF LOST SOULS
## BY AARON SMITH

Prelude: Atlanta, Georgia 1940

Everett Blaine was having one of his good days. He had managed to walk outside without falling. His aching old legs had done an admirable job with only a little help from his favorite cane. The flowers were in bloom and the Georgia sun felt warm on his wrinkled face. When a man makes it past his eightieth birthday, he takes all the good days he can get, not knowing how many more such days he might find before the clock runs out. The bad days came more often, but the good ones, the strong ones, were treasures to be savored. Up early, not a moment wasted, senses soaking in every detail, and as late to bed as possible, never sure if the next day will be another good one or a further step into the journey that will inevitably end in dust.

Blaine sat there in the garden from nine in the morning until nearly noon. He was about to get up, take the slow walk back to the house, hoping it would be as steady as the first journey had been, when a voice met his ears and told him that his good day had just become even better.

"Good morning, Granddaddy."

"Jeremy, my boy, I didn't expect to see you today!" Blaine smiled at the sight of his grandson emerging from between the bushes. The boy, just past his tenth birthday, looked just as his father had at that age and probably just as his grandfather had too, though Everett Blaine had never had his photograph taken at such an early age to be able to test that theory now.

"I had to come by, Granddaddy," Jeremy said, taking a seat on the garden bench beside the old man. "I have to ask you something. It's really important and I don't want to ask my father because he'll tell my mother all about it and she'll get to worrying about me and I don't want her getting upset."

"All right, Jeremy, what can I help you with?"

"Granddaddy," Jeremy said, his eyes pleading for an answer, "If I don't fight Bobby Bricker, does that mean I'm not a man?"

"Jeremy, why in heaven's name would you want to fight another boy?"

"Well, you see Granddaddy, he's been laughing at me and picking on me and yesterday when I told him to shut his big old mouth he came back and said to me that if I want to make him shut it I'm gonna have to fight him!

He said if I don't, it means I'm not a man. But the thing is, Granddaddy that I don't want to fight. Maybe I'm a coward because I'm afraid I might get hurt...and maybe it's something else: I'm kind of worried that I might hurt Bobby if we do fight, and I don't want to hurt anybody even if he is a big dumb mean kid! Am I a coward, Granddaddy? Is it true that I won't be a man if I don't fight Bobby tomorrow?"

Blaine laughed long and hearty, and then he grew quiet for a moment as the mists of memory clouded his mind, made him forget the warmth of the Georgia morning and the presence of his grandson. For an instant, he was far, far away from Atlanta, back in a place that was even hotter, in a time when he was not so old and, perhaps, he thought, not nearly as wise in the ways of the world.

Jeremy waited patiently until Granddaddy came back and then he heard the old man speak again.

"Jeremy, my boy, that little bully, Bobby Bricker, hasn't got the slightest idea what it means to be a man. I learned a very long time ago that a real man is one who does what needs to be done because it needs to be done, not because he has to prove a damn thing to anybody else or even to himself. There's no good reason for you to come to blows with that other boy and I hope you never do have a reason to come to blows with anybody in this life. But if you ever do have to fight for your life, Jeremy, and on that occasion you do what needs to be done, but only because you have no choice, then you'll grow up and be a man. Until then, why don't you just enjoy being a boy while it lasts? Have a good time, Jeremy, and don't be talked into doing anything foolish. Someday you may have to struggle to survive, but a thing like that is nothing to hope for, nothing to rush into. Trust me, son, I know."

Jeremy thought for a moment, admiring the way his grandfather always seemed to know exactly what he was talking about and answer his questions with the great honesty that comes from a lifetime of experience. Jeremy had to ask another question. His curiosity was now a fire burning a hole in his young mind.

"Granddaddy, how did you become a man?"

Everett Blaine hesitated. He wondered if it was a good idea to tell the story that had sprung into his mind at Jeremy's initial question. It was, Blaine knew, a dark story, brutal at times, frightening. But Jeremy was ten and he had the love of adventure that all healthy boys have, and there could be no harm in telling a healthy boy a great story. There was something else too, Blaine admitted to himself; it would do him good to relate the tale, for as harsh as the events of that time had been, he was young then, and it is always a good thing for an old man to feel young again, even if only in the echoes of his mind.

"Well, Jeremy, I suppose lunch can wait a while. I'll tell you a story…if you promise not to tell your mother, because she'll worry that it might give you nightmares!"

A story of which Mother would not approve is music to ten-year-old ears and so Jeremy Blaine was on the edge of his garden bench as his grandfather began to weave his tale.

"As you know, Jeremy, I was born right here in Atlanta in the year Eighteen-sixty. I've lived here most of my life, but did you know that I left here for several years when I was in my twenties? My father had been a Confederate officer. I don't remember the War Between the States, but I do recall that my father was considered a hero around here even if we did surrender to the damn Yanks at the end. Now when I was twenty-two years old and finished with my schooling and trying to decide what I was going to do with my life, my father had some business dealings with a solicitor in London, a retired British major called Holloway. There were some important papers that had to be sent to Major Holloway and my father just didn't trust the mail or even the expensive couriers you could hire to escort such documents overseas. So he sent me! I got on a ship and sailed clear across the Atlantic! Now that might not seem like such a big deal to you, Jeremy, in this modern age of airplanes, but back then a trip to England sounded like a grand adventure to a young man who'd never been away from the east coast of his own country before.

"I arrived in London safely, delivered those papers, and stayed with Major Holloway and his family for two weeks. The old soldier was a good man, loud and cheerful and full of colorful stories about his travels in Egypt and Afghanistan and other exotic places. His wife was a generous host, always making certain that her guests had everything they could possibly want.

"And then…then there was the Holloways' daughter. Gloria Holloway was the most perfect sight I'd ever seen and I think, even after all these years, still the most beautiful woman I've ever looked at. And the strange thing about it, Jeremy, was that Gloria didn't think I was such a bad thing to look at either! I couldn't get enough of her: that crisp, sweet accent of hers; that dark hair and pale skin; those deep, deep eyes that could swallow a man up if he looked into them for too long. I was in love, and I knew what I had to do.

"It took me three days of nervousness and three sleepless nights before I got up the gumption to do it. I swallowed my pride, marched straight into my host's study, and when he looked up from his paperwork to see who was there, I said, 'Major Holloway, I would like to ask for your daughter's hand in marriage.'

"Now, Jeremy, what do you think the major said to that?"

"What, Granddaddy?"

"Why, the old son of a bitch laughed at me! He looked up with a sneer in his expression and growled out in a voice that was far more serious than his usual tone and he said to me, 'Boy, you are not nearly man enough for my Gloria. You have never gone to war, never fired a shot in the clamor of battle, never fought for your life, never faced true hardship, never struggled to breathe your next breath or live another hour! You are a soft, spoiled child of a man and I would not give you the paw of my wife's poodle, much less my daughter's hand.'

"But then the old major realized what he'd said and regretted it. 'Everett, my boy,' he said then, 'I don't mean to offend you, for I do think you're a fine young man, but I will accept only the best for my daughter, and you have not yet proven yourself to me or to the world. I am sorry.'

"Well I was heartbroken for about a minute, Jeremy, and then my guts came back and I made up my mind that I wasn't about to let it rest at his refusal to grant me what I wanted. And so I asked, 'Well, Major Holloway, what can I do to prove to you that I'm up to the challenge of being your son-in-law? I'll do anything, sir!'

"He sat there for a minute scratching his beard and then he got a strange look in his eyes, the kind of look a poet gets when he's inspired, and he laughed. When he was done laughing he made me an offer. 'Everett, my boy, I was talking, a few days ago, with my old army friend Captain Dewsbury. Dewsie—that's what we used to call him, though try to forget that since he won't like being called that by anybody who didn't fight beside him in the desert—was telling me how he's heading back to Africa in a week to lead a hunting expedition. Everett, if I can get Dewsie to take you along on his little excursion into the jungle, and you can bring me home the head of a lion, then I might consider letting you have my Gloria. What do you think of that, son?'

"Well, Jeremy, my head spun around in a circle then and I had grand visions of green jungles and fierce lions and a joyful hunt and flying bullets and great adventure in mysterious faraway lands and my triumphant homecoming and my wedding to Gloria Holloway and the wedding night and…well, never mind that last part, I'll get in enough trouble telling you this story without that last part."

Jeremy was breathless now, the anticipation building. "So you went to Africa, Granddaddy? Did you shoot a lion as soon as you got there?"

"No, Jeremy," Everett Blaine said, "the first thing I did when I got off the ship at the Colony of Natal was get sick…sicker than I've ever been in my entire life."

Africa 1883

Everett Blaine's fever broke and he opened his eyes. His thirst was desperate, throat parched, lips dry. He coughed.

"Welcome back to the world."

The voice was deep, with English and something else combined in the accent. Blaine sat up, head still spinning though not too fast, and looked at the source of the words. A fat black man sat at Blaine's bedside, smiling, offering a cup.

Blaine drank fast, the cool water soothing away the sandpaper hurt of his mouth. "Who are you? Where am I?"

"The men here call me Ben," the giver of water said. "You would have some difficulty if you were to try to say the name my father gave to me! As for where you are, this is the hospital used by the British here in the colony. Perhaps you do not remember your arrival here in Africa, for you did not walk for long on these shores before the sickness took you away from us."

"How long have I been asleep?"

"A full week," Ben answered. "In the beginning, it was thought that you would not survive."

"An entire week lost?" Blaine was flabbergasted. "Where is Captain Dewsbury?"

"Mr. Blaine, I am sorry to tell you that your party has gone off into the jungle without you. They could delay the hunt no longer."

"Damn it all!" Blaine felt like everything he had come to Africa for had been blown to bits. He had missed the hunt, the lions, and the chance to bring his trophy home and win his bride. Even worse, he realized, old Major Holloway would think even less of him now, felled by some strange fever the moment he stepped off the boat, his weak constitution having betrayed him when he needed his strength the most.

"The doctor said I should bring you some supper when you woke," Ben said, getting up from his chair. He disappeared into the hall, leaving

Blaine alone to ponder his misfortune.

Alone now, Blaine let loose a stream of profanities that would have made almost anyone blush, words his mother back home in Atlanta would never have dreamed he even knew. He pulled the blankets back and swung his legs over the edge of the bed, intent on getting up, moving about if only to make his frustration less by way of physical activity. As soon as he sat up, his head began to spin, weakness and hunger knocking him back down again. He retreated, head sinking into the pillow, nausea dangerously close to erupting.

"Rising to your feet is a very bad idea, Mr. Blaine. A man's first bout with the fever that strikes down newcomers to Africa can be a hard thing. You don't want to tax yourself. You have to rest!"

Blaine reopened his eyes just enough to squint and see who had entered his room now. The voice was not Ben's. He expected a different orderly or a doctor. He found neither. The man who stood there was older, perhaps in his fifties, not very tall. He was small and wiry but in a strong way, a man toughened by many seasons under the hot African sun, skin once white but now bronzed and hard like the hide of some beast that had lived through many dangerous times, always managing to struggle through the fire and survive. He wore a wide-brimmed hat designed to shield the face and neck from the sun's wrath, a tan shirt with its sleeves rolled up to reveal tightly muscled forearms and calloused hands, trousers patched in several spots, and boots that must have been worn on many travels through thick brush and hot sands. The visitor's face was at once harsh and kind, tough and wise, not the face of a scholar but of one who had learned his lessons through vast and terrible experience. His eyes were bright and intelligent like those of a born predator and his beard was made up of half-inch long, bristly white hairs.

Blaine chanced another movement, slowly this time, carefully sitting up just enough to rest on his elbows, his head inches above the pillow, his stomach beginning to settle though still annoyed by pangs of hunger. "Do I know you, sir?"

"No," the man said, taking off his hat to reveal hair as white as that of his beard. "But I'm here under an obligation to keep watch over you until the matter of your health is settled."

"And how," Blaine asked, "did this duty fall upon your shoulders, sir?"

"Captain Dewsbury is an old acquaintance of mine, Mr. Blaine, and I've owed him a favor for some time now. Since you're under his charge and he had to go off on his hunt, he asked if I wouldn't mind seeing to your well-being until such time as you're well enough to set sail back to England or America or wherever you'll go from here."

"But," Blaine argued, "I don't wish to go back to either London or Atlanta! I have things I must do here in Africa! My...my future happiness depends upon it!"

"Settle down, son. You need to eat and rest. Once you've got your strength back, we can discuss this further."

At that moment, the orderly, Ben, came back with a tray of food which he set down on the bed across Blaine's legs. "Here you go. The doctor said to tell you not to eat it overly quick or you might send it right back onto its plate!"

As Blaine took a sip of the tea that had come with his meal, his visitor put his hat back on and gave a joking half-bow. "I'll be in the general area, Mr. Blaine. When the doctor gives his permission for you to be up and about, be sure to come and find me and we'll talk over a drink."

"But, sir," Blaine shouted as the very tan white man began to leave the room, "how will I find you?"

"Everybody 'round here knows me by name...and by reputation, whether the good one or the bad. Just ask, Mr. Blaine, and somebody will point you in the proper direction. The name is Quatermain. Now get some rest, boy!"

So that, Everett Blaine thought as he slowly filled his belly and felt his strength start to return, was Allan Quatermain! He had heard the name spoken again and again as the men he had sailed to Africa with, most of them old soldiers or experienced hunters who had been there before, told their tales to pass the time on the open sea.

This Quatermain, Blaine had learned, had quite a reputation as a hunter, adventurer, mercenary, explorer, and perhaps a scoundrel if some of the more colorful of the stories were true. Blaine chuckled as he recalled how, upon hearing the tales told aboard ship, he had imagined a much taller man than the real Quatermain, perhaps broad-shouldered and ageless and handsome. But, he decided as he finished his meat and set to work on the potatoes, perhaps the man called Quatermain would prove to be more interesting than the myth of the same name.

Blaine tried once more to get out of bed that evening, but Ben firmly prevented it, threatening to simultaneously sit on the patient and use his loud, booming voice to summon the doctor. Blaine gave up and fell asleep.

Blaine woke in the morning feeling like a new man. He rolled out of bed, dressed, and walked out of the hospital. The doctor had argued that he should spend one more precautionary day in bed, but Blaine felt too good, too strong to remain cooped up like a sick child. He strolled out of the building and into the clear, warm African morning, the busy streets of the Natal colony waiting for him to see for the first time with healthy eyes.

Sitting on the coast of south-east Africa, the area had been named a British colony forty years earlier in 1843. Now overseen by its governor, Sir Henry Ernest Gascoyne Bulwer, the colony had grown into a sprawling community with a startling mixture of British-style buildings and African-style dwellings intermixed like a garden sprouting two very different varieties of flowers. The populace was stunning in its contrast too as black and white, native and immigrant mingled, some conflict present between the races as tends to happen in such places, but people of many different origins and nationalities thriving in one way or another.

As Blaine began to walk about the area around the hospital, he could hear many languages being spoken: English, French, Dutch, Zulu and other Bantu languages, and various Indian dialects. People went about their business, the contrast between one person and another sometimes amazing to Blaine as he saw Europeans covered in the latest fashions of Paris walking along the same streets as natives just a stitch away from nakedness. There were tough looking men, soldiers or warriors of either race; women carrying children often with slightly older children trailing behind and laughing as they ran; horses strode by too, some pulling carts or wagons and others carrying single riders. The place was loud and bright and very, very hot. Dust kicked up from the ground as people and animals moved about and Blaine, taking it all in, realized how very far from Georgia he was. He had some money he had brought with him from London, so he would want for nothing, but he had no idea what he would do with the time that had suddenly fallen into his hands due to his being left behind by Captain Dewsbury's party. He decided to seek out Allan Quatermain, for he knew no one else in Africa.

"Good morning, Mr. Blaine! You feel good now, I see!"

It was Ben. The orderly approached with a big grin on his face.

"Ben," Blaine said, "perhaps you can help me. I'm looking for Mr. Quatermain, the man who visited me last night around the time you brought me my food. Do you have any idea where I might find him?"

"Yes, sir, he's been working with some of the English soldiers teaching them how to shoot better. Most days, he goes out to the edge of the settlement and hollers and yells and tells them what horrible shots they are until they get it right. When they hit the targets without wasting too many bullets, Macumazahn gets a big smile on his face and tells them all they're not as bad as he said a minute earlier!"

"Macoomaa…"

"Macumazahn," Ben repeated, slower now for Blaine's benefit. "That is what the Zulus call Quatermain. It means 'Watcher-by-night,' for the great hunter has been known to wake when other men sleep and to hear things which no other man can catch with his ears and also to see through the darkness with eyes as sharp as daggers. The senses of Quatermain are keen and dangerous and perhaps that is why he can shoot like no other man ever seen here in these lands."

"Interesting," Blaine said. "And how, Ben, would I get to this place where the soldiers hone their shooting skills?"

Ben wasted no time. He hollered and flagged down a passing wagon driven by a thin native with bushy gray hair. He muttered in something other than English.

"For a small price in English money," Ben turned to Blaine, "this fellow will drive you to the range. It is but a short while out of his way."

"Thank you, Ben." Blaine nodded and hopped into the wagon. The driver snapped the reins and the horses began to pull again. Blaine coughed a bit from the dust kicked up by eight trotting hooves. He hoped the drills would still be in session when he arrived, for he wanted to see if Quatermain really was as good a shot as he had heard from Ben and from the men aboard the ship on which he had come to Africa.

Blaine was not disappointed. The driver dropped him off at the edge of a wide field beyond the perimeter of the main part of the colony. British soldiers had gathered there, perhaps two dozen of them. Hundreds of feet from where the troops stood, targets had been set up, wooden sheets stood upright with patterns in the shapes of men painted on them with circles drawn in red where the heart and head would be. A sergeant and two privates were taking shots as Blaine arrived. The sergeant did fairly well, hitting the target just to the left of the heart while the first private just managed to nick the left shoulder of the stationary portrait. The third soldier fared poorly, his shot sailing right over the target and striking a tree in the distance.

Blaine watched as Allan Quatermain stomped over to the three shooters, waved the sergeant away, and bellowed at the two privates, "You boys ought to do better than that by now! Give me one of those!"

Quatermain tore the rifle from the hands of the man who had failed, lifted it and aimed. "Son, you have to see the bullet hitting home before you pull the trigger! Don't over think it. Feel the wind and let your eyes judge the distance and trust your instincts!"

Quatermain squeezed. A sharp crack was heard, and then a second crack as the wooden man took it right through the front of the painted-on skull.

"Now try it again!" Quatermain said, shoving the rifle back at the private.

The troops went back to practice as Quatermain stepped away, walked over to a parked wagon laden with guns and ammunition and other supplies. He picked up a canteen and drank deeply, wiping his lips with his sleeve when he finished.

"Good morning," he said as he saw Everett Blaine approach.

"Mr. Quatermain."

"Glad to see you up and about. What do you think of Africa now that you've seen some of it with eyes not hazed by fever?"

Blaine looked around. He stared up into the clear blue sky with its blazing sun, glanced down at the green and brown grass at his feet, looked off to the west where the jungle began and the peaks of mountains stuck up above the tree line to kiss the distant clouds.

"I think Africa is magnificent, Mr. Quatermain."

"And what do you intend to do now, Blaine?"

"Perhaps I could join another hunt," Blaine said, "since I seem to have missed the opportunity to be a part of Captain Dewsbury's expedition. Do you know of any others planning such a journey beyond the settlement?"

"Do you think you can shoot well enough to succeed on such a hunt?"

"I can shoot, Mr. Quatermain, though not like you if your demonstration here today is any indication."

"Show me," Quatermain said, picking up one of the rifles from the wagon and handing it to Blaine. The two men walked over to the range, where the troops had stopped for a rest and some water. "That third target hasn't seen a scratch yet by the miserable attempts of these unskilled boys. Make your mark, Blaine."

Blaine raised the rifle, thought back to the times his father, the old Confederate, had taken him into the lands outside Atlanta to shoot at empty whiskey bottles. He squinted through the light of the African sun

*"…the bullet cracked the target where the ribs would have been…"*

and took aim. He shot. The result was not perfect, but the shattering of wood was heard and the bullet cracked the target where the ribs would have been on a real man, two inches below the heart.

"Not the worst shot I've seen, Blaine," Allan Quatermain said. "You have a chance to take down a lion or a gazelle if you ever should find your way into a hunting party. Try again if you like."

Blaine let the rifle fall to his side. "Perhaps I'll shoot again tomorrow, Mr. Quatermain. I should like to see more of the colony today. Will you join me for a drink this evening?"

Quatermain never got the chance to answer. The soldiers around the shooting range all suddenly sprang to their feet at once, jumping to attention and raising their hands in salute. Blaine turned to see what had signaled the abrupt formality. A tall, stern-faced man in uniform had walked in among the troops, a colonel, Blaine saw by the insignia on the man's uniform.

"At ease, men," the officer roared. "Quatermain, I must speak with you immediately!"

"Colonel Huffington," Quatermain said. He turned to Blaine. "A pompous one this man is, but a good leader in battle, I've heard. If he's looking for me, he wants something, as he normally doesn't approve of my kind."

"We must speak alone, Quatermain," Huffington insisted.

"Excuse me, Blaine." Quatermain followed the colonel to a spot on the grass midway between the soldiers and the targets. Blaine watched, unable to hear the words at that distance, as the officer and the old hunter talked. Huffington waved his arms to accentuate whatever he had to say, while Quatermain stood still and took it all in, nodding once or twice to indicate his understanding. Minutes later, Huffington finished, turned and walked back the way he had arrived, the enlisted British all rising and saluting again as the colonel departed.

Quatermain walked back over to where Blaine waited.

"Blaine, we shall have to delay that drink. The colonel has requested my advice and possibly my aid and I may have to leave the colony for a time."

"Is something wrong?" Blaine asked. "Has something happened?"

"Some fools, it seems," Quatermain said, "have underestimated the dangers of Africa and run off to get themselves killed or worse! Women! Always it's women who do the silliest, most dangerous things in places they have no business being to begin with! And then it falls to men to go and pull their hides out of the fire! That's how it always is, Blaine. There ought to be a decree to keep them from setting foot on this continent, no matter how shining and pure their foolish intentions are!"

Quatermain stormed away, still grumbling to himself. Blaine watched him go but soon felt an irresistible urge to follow. He had to know precisely what had happened. Curiosity got the best of him and he took off running after Quatermain.

Quatermain hopped onto a wagon driven by a British corporal, shot off on the road back into the center of the colony. Blaine ran after, yelling, begging for the driver to wait for him. Almost out of breath, the young American caught up, hopped into the back of the wagon, panting and wheezing, taking a position across from Quatermain.

"What exactly has happened, Mr. Quatermain? Is there something I can do to help?"

"Let me be, Blaine. I have no time to watch over you now, despite the favor I owe Dewsbury."

"I'm not asking for a governess," Blaine argued. "I simply wish to know what Colonel Huffington said to cause you to go rushing off with such urgency. What's all this about women in danger?"

"Bloody hell," Quatermain spat. "I might as well tell you about it on the way." The old hunter took his pipe from his pocket and fumbled with a match to light it as the wagon rumbled along the unpaved road. Three hearty puffs of tobacco smoke later, he told Blaine what he knew so far.

"Some people seem to think, Blaine, that the simple act of doing the lord's work will protect them from all perils along the way. I wonder how many fools have died because of that assumption over the centuries! In all my years in Africa, I've seen it happen more than once. People back in England or in America or France or anywhere else in the world read novels about Africa and dream about the mystery and drama of it all but they don't have an idea of the dangers out there once you travel beyond the settlements! The deserts and the jungles are no place for soft-bodied people with no wits and no experience. Women especially! But they've gone and done it again!"

"Done what, Mr. Quatermain?" Blaine grew impatient as Quatermain rambled.

"A flock of Englishwomen," Quatermain explained, "all of them having graduated from some exclusive women's college, and all hell-bent on converting the 'poor ignorant natives' to Christianity, arrived here by boat some weeks ago. At first, according to Colonel Huffington, they were content to flitter about the colony and lead their prayer meetings and teach hymns to those Zulus who have picked up some English. But that wasn't enough for these ladies, it seems, and they felt the urge to go off and find the real 'heathens' and work on them too…so they trotted off into the jungle despite the advice of any man who knows anything about Africa. Yes, Blaine, they truly were that foolish! Ten Englishwomen accompanied only by six native guides, trudging off into the thick of the wild armed with bibles and good intentions! The sheer stupidity of it astounds me!"

"Let me guess," Blaine said. "They haven't been heard from and now you're expected to go with the colonel as a guide to try and find them."

"Oh no, Blaine," Quatermain shook his head sadly, "they have been heard from…at least one of them has! It seems one of those young ladies came crawling to one of the outposts not far from the edge of the colony last night. She had dragged herself for miles, naked and starving and with an arrow through her shoulder! They've got her at the hospital now and they're hoping she can speak soon and relate what happened to the rest of her party before she goes insane from the shock of it or dies from infection! But you were partly correct, Blaine. What the good colonel wants is for me to take some of his men out that way and either find the rest of those women and bring them back to civilization…or recover whatever is left of them for a good, decent burial!"

"I see," Blaine said, shaking his head at the horror of the situation. "When do you intend to leave on this quest?"

"The colonel has asked that I meet him at the hospital at noon to see if any information can be gotten from the injured girl. Perhaps she can provide some clue as to which direction the missionaries traveled in. If we can choose a likely route, we shall leave as soon as tomorrow morning."

"Quatermain…I volunteer to go along!"

"No, Blaine! There is no reason for you to risk your own life!"

"But I can be of some help I think."

"You know nothing of the jungle, son."

"Back home, I often went hunting in the forests. Can the jungle be so different, so much more perilous?"

"That you would ask me that, Blaine…shows how little you know of Africa!"

"But Quatermain, I have already shown you that I can shoot, perhaps not as well as you, but surely accurately enough to be of use in a fight! And there are defenseless women out there. I cannot just sit idly in comfort and allow you, who I have come to think of as a friend and an honorable man, to charge off into danger. And furthermore, my reason for coming to this place was to prove something, to earn the respect of a man on whose opinion of me hangs the fate of my future happiness. If I cannot bring him the head of a lion as he requested, then perhaps I can earn his favor by assisting you in this endeavor."

"Blaine, I admire your courage even if it only shows through in words thus far, but you are only just recovered from a fever that almost ended your life!"

"I have my strength back now, Quatermain. I feel as though I could run for miles at this very moment. At least let me accompany you to see the patient. After that, depending on what she says, you can decide if I should go with you or remain behind."

Quatermain took a long puff on his pipe, stared at Blaine for a long time as if drawing up an estimation of the younger man's mettle. Finally, he cleared his throat and spoke.

"I suppose, Blaine, that every man must earn his stripes at some point. How old are you?"

"I am twenty-three, sir."

"I suppose that's old enough to know whether or not you're willing to place your neck on the block for a gaggle of silly geese! All right, Blaine. If you're so insistent, I'll let you come along, but I will not serve, as you said before, as your governess! The jungle is tough and a man who wants to survive its grasp has got to be tougher. I hope you understand what you're getting yourself into."

The two men, one an old hunter and trader, and the other just come to the strange continent of Africa, shook hands as the wagon rattled into the more heavily populated part of the colony at Natal.

❋ ❋ ❋

Blaine was almost toppled by a combination of rage and nausea as he and Quatermain entered the hospital room and got their first sight of the unfortunate young woman who had emerged from the harsh lands outside the borders of the colony. He had to look away, stare at the wall for a moment before gathering the courage to go back for a second viewing. Allan Quatermain, Blaine noticed, seemed unfazed by the horror before them, as if he had been numbed by many terrible sights over many difficult years. But Quatermain's clenched fist began to tremble at his side and Blaine saw that as a sign that the old explorer was more affected by the woman's state than his face showed.

The patient was unconscious. Her face was a mess, red and blistered from facing the sun with no protection. Her shoulders and arms, exposed while the rest of her body was covered by the blanket, were bruised, scratched and torn. One shoulder was heavily bandaged with cloth that had been white but was now stained both with blood and with the ointments smeared on the wound to treat infection.

"I doubt she will wake," said Quatermain.

"You are, I fear, correct," a doctor said, entering the room. "She was conscious for several hours when she arrived here, but has since fallen back into a stupor of shock. The infection in her wound is too much for my powers to deal with. She does not have long to live. Perhaps we will never learn what befell her companions."

"There must be something you can do!" Blaine shouted.

"Please be quiet," the doctor scolded. "There are other patients here who need their rest. The abilities of physicians are limited and sometimes we lose our battles."

"It is unfortunate," Quatermain added, "but this is how life in these harsh lands often ends, Blaine. Let us leave this room and let the girl pass from this world when she can fight no longer."

The three men walked out into the hallway. Blaine was angry, distraught. Quatermain, no stranger to tragic sights and circumstances, was calm and thoughtful. He turned to the physician.

"Doctor, what became of the arrow you removed from the girl's shoulder?"

"I have it in my office waiting to be collected with the rest of the rubbish when the next shift of orderlies comes on duty. Why do you ask?"

"May I see it?"

"Yes, of course."

In the office, the doctor fished into a bin holding an assortment of trash and produced the two parts of a broken arrow. The projectile had been snapped halfway up the shaft. Quatermain took both pieces from the doctor and looked them over, examining the bloodstained head, the middle shaft section, and finally the fletching of feathers at the end of the rear segment of the arrow.

He held the pieces up near the window, using the sunlight to illuminate the inspection, cleared his throat several times as he peered closely at the objects, and finally turned to Blaine.

"This entire affair is not what it initially seemed to be, Blaine. Something is very unusual here!"

"What do you mean?"

"This is not the arrow of any of the tribes in this region. What I have here, Blaine, is what is left of a white man's arrow! Look at the feathers used for fletches! These were taken from a wood pigeon, a bird you'd never find in Africa! And this shaft was not shaped by any tool used by the Zulus of any other natives of this part of the world. Look at the head of this arrow, Blaine. No tribesman of the jungles here could create such a precise point on a metal arrowhead! This is one of a batch of arrows used by competitive archers in Europe! This was not made in Africa but more likely imported from England or Spain or France. Either one of the tribes in this region traded for or stole their arrows…or that poor dying girl was not shot by natives at all!"

"Then who was it that attacked the party of missionaries?" Blaine asked.

"Unless that young lady wakes and speaks before she dies," Quatermain said, "we shall only find the answer to that question in the lands beyond this colony! Come, Blaine, we have preparations to make!"

They set off that afternoon, having decided not to wait for the next morning. After seeing the state of the injured girl and having his curiosity enflamed by the surprising style of the arrow, Quatermain had gone straight to Colonel Huffington, Blaine following close behind, and insisted that the search party be dispatched at once.

There would be nine men going into the jungle, fewer than Quatermain wanted, but Huffington claimed he could spare only four soldiers, and no officers, so that the army presence on the hunt would consist only of a sergeant called Brant and three privates. There would be three natives along as well, two hired to carry supplies and the hospital orderly Ben, who volunteered for the mission on the grounds that he felt sorry for the girl who had crawled back to the colony and he wanted to be there if justice would be delivered to her attackers. Blaine at first wondered why the heavyset Ben would be allowed to come along, as a man of that size would surely slow the party down, but Quatermain explained that Ben was capable of faster movement than one might assume at first glance and that he had been a brave and resourceful warrior in his younger days.

So they set off: Quatermain, Blaine, three Zulus, and four British soldiers. Their rations load consisted of several days' worth of water and food, plenty of tobacco, and bandages and medicines given to them by the hospital should they find any injured survivors or sustain any wounds themselves. As for weapons, there would be a rifle each for Quatermain, Blaine, each soldier, and Ben. The two servants carried their own weapons: daggers and spears which they strapped to their backs to free their hands to carry supplies. Quatermain also brought his personal pistol, which he tucked into his belt, as well as a large skinning knife which he had, over the years, used for dismantling animals he had hunted, preparing food, and occasionally killing a man in battle. They would journey on foot, the thick undergrowth of the jungle no place for horses or other beasts of burden and transport.

Wagons driven by British troops carried the party as far as the edge of the Natal colony. There, the nine men were deposited to carry on without assistance. They began the march across a flat, grassy plain toward the thick jungle that began several miles to the west.

As they walked, Everett Blaine looked around and saw two things at once: with his eyes he admired the natural splendor of Africa, but in his mind he could still see the pitiful condition of the poor dying girl. For the first time since offering to go along on the trek, he felt real fear forming in his gut. He glanced over at Allan Quatermain and was at least partially consoled by the knowledge that his companion had many years of experience and had faced and lived through so many jungle-born dangers. Blaine hoped his luck would make up for what he lacked in experience, hoped he would manage to live as long as Quatermain had.

They made good time reaching the line where the plain ended and the thick forest began. At the border, all nine men stood and stared into the seemingly endless mass of tree-covered land before them as if they were about to walk into the bowels of Hell. The three natives made strange signs with their hands as if trying to ward off evil before it attacked. The soldiers mumbled prayers of their own. Everett Blaine just looked, wondering what lay in store for them beyond the natural division between open air and dense jungle. It was Allan Quatermain who ran out of patience first and urged them on.

"Praying will do us no good, gentlemen, and we haven't the time to waste! This is where we leave God behind and walk on our own into the fire. Be alert and keep your eyes and ears open...but do not react until you're certain we face danger! There's no sense wasting ammunition unless a threat is real and not some imagined phantom. Let's leave superstition where it belongs and act like men! Forward!"

They entered the jungle. Quatermain led the way, followed by Blaine and Sergeant Brant. Behind the front men the three lower-ranked soldiers and the three Zulus went on in no particular order, for marching drills were irrelevant in the jungle, where one often had to shift course to the left or the right to avoid vines or roots that might snag the feet and send a man face first to the ground.

"This," said Sergeant Brant "is near to the area where our patrols spotted the girl as she crawled out of the jungle. We must find the trail if we can."

"Let me," said Quatermain, holding up his hands to halt the others. He began to stalk carefully about the brush, looking down at the ground. "All of you remain here for a moment." He went forward alone, vanishing into the thick jungle ahead of the rest of the party.

Blaine and the others stood and waited. The young American listened to the sounds of the jungle, remembering how far from familiar Georgia he was. He could hear a far-off chattering sound, perhaps apes of some sort. Birds squawked and cawed overhead as they flitted from treetop to treetop. All else was quiet. It was hot, but not as unbearable as the plain between colony and jungle had been, for the trees provided good cover and kept out the harshest of the sun's rays. Blaine took a sip from his canteen.

"Come along now!" Quatermain's voice cut the silence after several minutes. Sergeant Brant waved the others forward and they moved to catch up to their scout.

Blaine, Brant, and Ben stood with Quatermain in a circle around some shrubs that had been mashed into the ground, as if depressed by weight for a long time.

"Something the size of that young lady stopped here for long enough to destroy this section of the brush," Quatermain said. "It looks as though she dragged herself along the path leading to this spot, as I can see that the ground-cover is flattened to some degree as it stretches back further into the jungle. Then she stopped here, perhaps needing a rest, trying to regain her strength to continue on. It seems we've found our trail. We go single-file from here. I shall lead. Blaine, you come next, for I'll show you things along the way, give you a proper African education! Sergeant, arrange the rest of the line as you see fit."

They travelled on for miles more but the sun fell low in the sky and the shadows took dominance over the light and the time for walking was done for the day. A fire was lit in the center of a small clearing and the men sat around it, ate, talked until dusk gave way to full dark, and then lay down on the ground to sleep, eight at a time with each man standing watch for an hour shift.

Everett Blaine found it difficult to fall asleep, having never been in the jungle before, let alone tried to rest in its intimidating darkness. He lay there with his eyes shut and listened to the sounds of the breeze moving the leaves on the tall trees, the cries of faraway nocturnal beasts, and the loud snoring of one of the soldiers. When he finally drifted off, his slumber was soon interrupted by a nudge to his shoulder.

"It's your turn now," whispered Sergeant Brant.

Blaine stood and stretched and began to pace, quietly as possible, around the perimeter of the campsite. He ventured a few feet into the jungle but just far enough to feel a shiver, not from any cold, for it was quite warm there even at night, but from the eeriness of the strange environment. As he turned to walk back to the fireside, the tip of his boot struck something hard which rolled a few inches. He thought it was a rock, but the sound was somehow wrong, hollower than the noise a kicked stone would have made. He bent down, picked it up, and strolled back to the light to examine it. As the glow met the object, Blaine let out a cry of shock, dropped the thing to his feet.

"Quatermain, look at this!"

Allan Quatermain, as readily as if he had not been asleep at all, jumped up from the ground, displaying agility beyond what one would expect from a man of his age, and ran to Blaine.

"What is it?"

"There, Quatermain, on the ground. I do not wish to touch it again!"

Quatermain had no such hesitation. He bent down and lifted the round, smooth, utterly fleshless human skull that his young companion had discovered.

"This," the old hunter said, "has not been here long despite its being entirely stripped of its skin and hair. Maggots have eaten away the eyes and, judging by the lack of weight, the brain as well."

The others began to wake. Ben, the hospital man, approached and stared at the skull.

"Look at the place where it was struck from the neck, Macumazahn. That was done by a sharp sword, not by the crude ax or knife of a tribesman. You were correct in what you said about the arrow. This poor soul was killed by white man weapons!"

Attempts to sleep would have been futile after the grim discovery. The nine men sat around the fire and talked until first light, then got up and resumed their trek, wondering if more corpses or pieces of them would be found.

It did not take long for bones to appear in grisly abundance.

"Dear lord!" shouted Sergeant Brant as he nearly tripped over a pile of human remains, just regaining his balance in time.

The entire party stopped, looked around. The carnage sent them into breathless awe. Bodies lay all around them, some stripped to bones by whatever carnivorous beasts had come across the scene prior to its discovery, others still partially covered in decaying flesh. One corpse was headless and the searchers knew they had already met its top piece by the campfire in the night.

"The six native guides!" Quatermain said. "These are all bodies of men."

One body was pinned to a tree by an arrow through the neck. Several others wore the telltale marks of swords having penetrated ribcages. All had died horrible, agonizing deaths.

"But what has become of the women?" Everett Blaine asked.

"Clearly, they were taken away by whatever monstrous manner of men did *this*!" As Quatermain spoke he waved his arm in the direction of the dead, disgust and rage evident on his face.

The two servants began to make a terrible noise. Quatermain went over to them, began to speak in the Zulu language, in which he was fluent. Debate went back and forth and finally Quatermain threw his hands up in anger and cried out, in English now, "So be it, you bloody cowards!"

At that, the two men who had carried the party's rations to that point in the jungle dropped their loads and turned and ran back in the direction from which they had come.

"What the devil was that about?" Sergeant Brant asked.

"They said the few coins they're paid for travelling with us are not enough for them to have to face demons," Quatermain explained. He turned to the British privates. "You men will have to take up the task of carrying our supplies."

"Actually, sir," the sergeant interrupted, "it is my opinion that whoever killed these poor chaps outnumbers us significantly enough that we really ought to go back and fetch reinforcements before we proceed with this hunt."

Quatermain spit on the ground. "You would turn tail and run too, Brant? Cowards: the whole lot of you! Those women were not slain here; do you not understand what that means? They may still be alive! Will none of you go forward with me and see if we can save them?"

"I will," said Everett Blaine.

"And so will I, Macumazahn!" Ben added. "After what happened to that poor woman at the hospital, I wish to help you kill these villains, no matter how great their numbers!"

"Very well then," Quatermain said, watching as Brant and his men retreated. "Three of us against God-only-knows how many others; we shall have to go quietly then and use our brains and our wits rather than brute force if we are to succeed against such odds. We will take our canteens and as much food as we can carry without being too weighed down. Our weapons, of course, are our most important possessions now that we have seen the savagery of those we pursue. Forward!"

❋ ❋ ❋

Several hours later, the three men stopped to rest. They had walked through miles of thick jungle and seen nothing else of note save for the signs of travel in large numbers, the pressed down brush and broken shrubbery that Quatermain followed with unerring tracking skills. They had not spoken much either, all shocked by the flight of their six companions.

"How do you feel, Blaine?" Quatermain asked as he sat on a rock and filled his pipe.

"Well enough, I suppose. Why do you ask?"

"Because you, young friend, are unaccustomed to these lands and yet you remained on the trek while the soldiers ran off. Courage, son, is an admirable trait, but I hope your reasons are not foolish ones. Is this young lady in England worth the risk you've chosen to take by continuing our quest?"

"Any danger, Mr. Quatermain, is worth facing if it wins me the woman I love!"

Quatermain sighed. "To be young and in love, Blaine, is no insurance against doom, although I surely wish it were so."

"You have survived many challenges in Africa, Quatermain. Why should I not be so lucky?"

"I, my boy, have Africa in my blood. Superstitious as this may sound to foreign ears…this place is on my side. I am a part of Africa and it is a part of me. Can you say the same for yourself?"

"All I can say, Quatermain, is that I am doing what I feel I must. Would you try to convince me to go back as the others have?"

"That, Blaine, is not my decision to make. Now eat while we have these few moments. Soon we must go forth and use what hours of daylight remain."

*"Three of us against God-only-knows…"*

Quatermain smoked and Blaine ate just enough to fill his stomach without weighing him down or making him too content or drowsy. Ben had wandered off to relieve himself. As Blaine washed down his food with a long swig from his canteen, Ben came rushing back into sight shouting.

"Macumazahn! Macumazahn!"

"What is it?" Quatermain stood, dumped the ashes from his pipe.

"Come and see," Ben said, pointing into the jungle. "I have found something!"

The three men grabbed their rifles and gear and advanced.

"There!" Ben pointed.

Scattered on the jungle floor were heaps of cloth and scraps of paper and leather. Quatermain knelt down to examine the debris.

"This is clothing, Blaine! The remains of the outer garments of the nine remaining women! And these…" He picked up several of the torn sheets of paper that littered the ground, "Are pages torn from Bibles! Whoever took these women forced them to leave their symbols of civility behind, and harshly it seems, judging from the way these blouses and dresses were cut away from their wearers. By divesting them of their holy books as well, the brutes dehumanized them even further!"

"What sort of men are we tracking, Quatermain?" Blaine asked. "What monsters would treat helpless women in such ways?"

"This kind of men," Quatermain answered with anger boiling on his tongue, "are all too common in this wretched world! We must increase our speed and hope that worse crimes have not yet been committed against these women. It pains me to say this, but perhaps the luckiest of them was the poor girl who has surely perished by now in the hospital at Natal."

"At least we know we're on the right trail," Blaine said.

"Yes," Quatermain nodded. "Let's not linger here."

They continued on, still following the signs of passage, leaving the piles of torn clothing and books behind, all their minds filled with the horrors of what might be happening to the captive women.

After an hour more of trudging through thick brush, they stopped abruptly, surprised by the sight before them.

"A real trail," Ben said, "so far out here in the wild!"

The ground ahead was a smooth pathway, dirt only, as if many years of men travelling over the land had worn away the vegetation and cancelled out any hope of new growth.

"Interesting," Quatermain said. "The native tribes out this way make no such regular roads. Something is very odd about this. Still, this strange find will make our tracking all the easier. But be alert, men. On a path as well-traveled as this one, there may be eyes in the trees and off to our sides. We, the seekers, may now be the watched!"

Quatermain and his two companions travelled on for many hours, following the dirt path. On both sides the jungle was thick and green. The men were on the alert for any signs of unusual activity, but saw or heard nothing that did not belong. There was no further indication of human activity. Everett Blaine, the least experienced of the three, was startled a few times by animal noises, which sent Ben into fits of laughter, but the trek was otherwise uneventful. They walked until dark and set up camp again, huddled around a small fire to eat and smoke and rest.

They filled their bellies, still possessing adequate food for several days' journey, provided they did not overeat. After supper, Quatermain puffed on his pipe, Ben fell asleep first and began to snore, and Blaine sat and stared into the shadows, growing tired of waiting and wishing something would happen soon to break the terrible suspense.

"How can you stand this damned silence, Quatermain?"

"One of the first lessons you must be taught, young man," Quatermain said, "is that in the jungle, silence is your friend. Now it is quiet in the night and that makes you uneasy, but would you rather have the silence broken by the roar of a hungry lion or the stampeding feet of elephants that would trample you to dust or the hiss of a snake about to strike? When all you can hear is the crackle of the firewood and the distant whisper of the wind, then you are mostly safe. It is sound that should upset you more than quiet, Blaine. Remember that well."

"I know you're right, Quatermain, but it's a difficult adjustment to make. Although I spent time in the woods of Georgia, the quality of the silence here is different, more unsettling in a way I find difficult to express in plain words."

"The jungle," Quatermain said, "often seems to have its own mind, a kind of consciousness that defies the way we ordinary men think of nature. Perhaps it is that very quality that has called to me my entire life and enticed me to stay in Africa even when opportunities have arisen to perhaps find a better, easier living in other sections of the world. It is here I belong, despite the dangers, despite the oddness of the place. Perhaps I am just an old man gone sentimental and less than sane, but that is how I feel about Africa."

Blaine laughed. "That was quite the dramatic speech, my friend. I will not pretend to fully understand your feelings, but perhaps I will when I have as many years experience in life as you do. You must have a great many stories you could relate of the trials you have faced in these weird lands, of the wonders…and horrors also…that you have witnessed."

"Yes," Quatermain said with a tired sigh, "but none that I care to tell tonight. Get some rest, Blaine. Perhaps Ben's snoring will drown out the quiet that disturbs you so and lull you to sleep."

Quatermain waited until he was certain Blaine had fallen asleep. He thought he had heard something else while he had been discussing the sounds of the jungle with Blaine, something in the background, a vibration that a man less knowledgeable about the jungle would surely have missed. He had not wanted to alarm the others, for they needed their rest. Now Quatermain was free to investigate.

He got up, left his rifle leaning against the large stone upon which he had sat while smoking, made sure his pistol was securely tucked into his belt, and took out his knife; if he was going to need a weapon at all, he decided, it would be the quiet one.

Slowly and cautiously, making barely a sound as he crossed the line that divided the little campsite from the jungle beyond, Quatermain advanced up the path, leaving his companions behind. His eyes, long practiced at peering through jungle darkness, made use of starlight in places where torches would be needed by other men. In the jungle, alone, Allan Quatermain stalked more like a beast than a man, not thinking in words, but letting his senses and instincts guide him onward.

There it was again! He stopped, stood, listened. What he thought he had heard earlier was the sound of drums, the beating, pounding rhythms of jungle music, but it had been different than the music that normally would have floated through the night air. The beat had been slurred, distant, not as if it had come from miles away, but like its source was close by yet in another world. His earlier feeling was now confirmed. The drums were being beaten, but Quatermain, despite all his years of experience in tracking, hunting, exploring, could suddenly not tell from which direction the sound was coming. Quatermain did not know what to make of the mystery, but that only magnified his determination.

As he walked on, guided by moonlight, Quatermain saw that the dirt roadway, which had been a more or less straight line for most of the day's journey, now curved off to the right. He followed, listening to the weird drumming that defied his attempts to pinpoint its location. Another ten minutes' walk and Quatermain stopped. The path had abruptly ended, coming to a halt at a stone wall some ten feet high, well enough above Quatermain's head that he could not see over it. It was wide too. From where he stood, Quatermain could not see either end of the wall, as if it stretched on for many feet, its furthermost edges vanishing into the darkness to his left and his right. Perplexed, he glanced at the ground, found a round stone the size of a man's fist, and threw it up at the top of the wall. He heard it bounce off the top of the wall but not come down on the other side, which indicated to him that it was not just a wall but a structure of some kind, a building he had not expected to come across in a jungle region where no such places had ever been, as far as he knew, erected. The tribes that populated these lands, Quatermain knew, tended to live in straw huts, so this place had to be from some previous population, forgotten by history.

Quatermain placed his ear against the wall, thinking that perhaps the drumming was coming from within the mysterious structure. No, he realized, it was not from inside. He could still hear it, but had no further clue as to its origin.

He cursed, frustrated. No more could be determined in the dark, he decided. He turned around and began to follow the dirt path back to the campsite. When dawn came, he would get a better look at the place.

"Macumazahn, I have had the strangest of dreams," said Ben as he woke to find Allan Quatermain enjoying a morning smoke. The sun was rising and the day growing bright. The birds had begun to chirp and the air was cool but growing warmer by the second.

"And what was that, Ben?"

"I dreamed that my ears were touched by the sound of drumming like none I have heard before in all my years, music with rhythm so strange and timing so unusual that I doubt any like it has ever been heard in Africa!"

"Lay your doubts aside," Quatermain said, "for I have heard such drumming in Africa…just this past night! You did not dream it, Ben, but truly heard such sounds, although they reached your mind through the clouds of sleep and so you believed it to be only a dream. The music was real!"

"But then where, Macumazahn, did it come from?"

"I tried to find that very answer while you slept, friend, but a great wall was in my way and I could not trace the drumming to its source. But now that day is here, we can try again, all three of us this time. Rouse young Blaine now and we shall be on our way."

In the pleasant morning warmth, the trek to the wall at the end of the path was a comfortable one. Blaine and Ben were well-rested and Quatermain, even not having slept, was alert and vigorous. They reached the wall in short time and stood staring.

"Good God, Quatermain, how did something like this get here?" Blaine asked, stunned by the apparent age of the structure.

"A remnant of some long-forgotten city, I would guess," Quatermain said. "Now that the sun has lit things up, I can see that this temple or whatever it is…or was…is round. See how it curves as it goes off to both our left and our right?"

"That is why we cannot see where it ends," Ben said. "Which way shall we go, Macumazahn?"

"I vote that we examine both directions at once and save time," Blaine suggested.

"Agreed," Quatermain nodded. "Blaine, go right and shout if you find an entrance or anything else of interest. I will follow the wall to the left. Ben, you remain here where you'll be able to listen for either of us and then call out to the other if one of us shouts. We will have the best communication that way."

They split then, Blaine nervous with his rifle held out as he walked, and Quatermain moving in a more relaxed manner but still ready as ever to respond to danger of any sort.

Everett Blaine was trying to get used to the jungle, trying his best to stay confident and calm, but he was wracked with doubt. Already he had seen a poor young woman dying because of whatever had happened out in those lands, and there had been the bodies, cut and shot and terrible to see, of the native guides. The other nine women were still missing and now this strange, seemingly ancient building had appeared in the path of the three searchers. Blaine was afraid, feeling very out of his element and very uncertain if he would ever make it back even to the Natal colony, let alone see his family back in Georgia or Gloria Holloway in London. As he followed the long, curving stone wall, he worried that he had thrown his life away to follow Allan Quatermain on this foolish crusade.

Allan Quatermain walked with confidence as he searched the long, curving stone wall for any sign of an entrance, but he was beginning to feel uneasy. He heard nothing, saw nothing to alarm him, but his instincts did not often fail him and he could feel danger close by. As often happened when a threat may have been near, some of his thoughts turned to the many dangers he had faced in the past and also to the things in his life that held value for him. He thought of his two wives, women he had not seen in what felt like ages, for they were of parts of his life that were long gone. He thought of his son Harry, off studying to become a doctor, a more noble profession than that of a hunter and trader. He thought too of the land of Africa with all its beauty and splendor and how much he loved it even if it had come close to costing him his life on many separate occasions. Then, realizing that his thoughts were beginning to wander, Quatermain dismissed his memories to focus on the present, to watch and listen and decide whether or not the danger he felt was real. The wall he examined looked solid as far as he could see, but he knew that no building could go on forever and assumed an entrance would be found before he had traversed the entire perimeter of the structure. He wondered how Blaine was faring in his walk around the area, wondered which of them would find the way in first.

Ben paced on the grassy ground in front of the wall. He yawned once. He listened to the sparse sounds of the jungle morning, the birds and breeze and small mammalian things that scampered among the brush. He gazed up at the clear blue sky that showed in patches between the treetops. He stopped walking around, leaned against the stone wall, and closed his eyes for a moment, wishing he had slept a bit longer. There was a sudden sound, an unexpected creaking. He felt himself fall backward and felt a pair of strong hands on his shoulders. Startled, Ben dropped his rifle, felt his hat fall from his head, and screamed.

※ ※ ※

At the sound of the scream, Quatermain drew his pistol and began to run back to the point where the three men had parted ways. His strong legs carried him quickly; he was agile and swift for a man of his age.

At the opposite end of the course taken by the split party, Blaine heard Ben's cry and responded as Quatermain had, running back and retracing his footsteps. Blaine's knuckles whitened as he gripped his rifle tight, wondering what danger had caused his Zulu friend to call out with such terror.

When Blaine arrived, Quatermain was already there. The old hunter stood holding Ben's hat; the dropped rifle was still on the ground. Ben was nowhere to be seen.

"What happened?" Blaine asked, catching his breath.

"I don't know," Quatermain said. "Ben is gone, but I can't see where he may have gone!"

"He let out a terrible cry!"

"Yes, Blaine, I heard it too, though it was not a cry of pain but one of shock, which means perhaps he is still alive."

"But where would he go and leave his gun behind? Ben is no fool!"

"Look around, Blaine," Quatermain said, pointing to the grass and to the trees. "The grass here is not trampled as if Ben had gone running from some threat. He did not leave here quickly on foot. I believe we can also assume that he was not carried off by some large bird! What does that leave?"

"Could it be, Quatermain that Ben is inside this mysterious structure which we have been unable to enter?"

"It would appear so." Quatermain stared at the wall for a moment then began running his hands over the surface of the stone. "Good Lord! Look closely, Blaine. There is indeed a seam here, as if this portion of the wall is a thick stone door. It must open from the inside, which means that the building is occupied and whoever is within has taken Ben!"

"Incredible! But Quatermain…how do we go after him? We cannot possibly move this heavy slab of stone from the outside."

"Yet there has to be a way in," Quatermain said, "for if men are within, they must have arrived there through some opening. We must continue our walk around the entire thing before we leap to any conclusions. This time we go together. I will conceal Ben's rifle behind that tree, the thick one. We can retrieve it later if need be."

❋ ❋ ❋

Nearly an hour later, they had found nothing. Quatermain and Blaine had traveled the entire perimeter of the ancient stone building. It was a large circle, solid all around, with a few seamed sections like the one where Ben had vanished, but no apparent way of entering from without. They stopped upon returning to the point at which the long walk had begun.

Shielding his eyes from the glare of the sun, Allan Quatermain looked up at the top of the wall. "We seem, Blaine, to have but one option left to us. If we cannot enter from the ground, perhaps our answer lies above. You are the taller man. Here, let me boost you up."

Using Quatermain's cupped hands as a step, Blaine reached up, gripped the top of the wall, and pulled himself up onto the roof of the structure. He stood, looked around at the flat stone top which was covered with many years of moss and ivy. He knelt down and let his rifle hang down over the edge, holding it tightly. Quatermain grabbed hold of the gun's long barrel and came up next, climbing like a little monkey of a man, strong legs against the wall, grunting and straining to keep his sideways balance. When both men were atop the mysterious old building, they began to look around, tearing up the plants that had taken root in the cracks.

"Over here!" Blaine shouted from the far end of the rooftop after the search had gone on for some time. Quatermain rushed over to join him there. Both men stood looking down into a small, square opening in the roof. Vines had grown over it but Blaine had now torn most of the green tentacles away. The sun shone down but not brightly enough to penetrate to the bottom of the hole.

"How far do you think the drop is, Quatermain?"

"The sound will tell us," Quatermain said. He had picked up the round stone he had thrown onto the roof when he had found the place in the night. He dropped it into the opening. An instant later, the impact was heard, stone striking stone. "Not more than ten feet, I would say. It seems the floor of the inside was laid flat upon the jungle ground."

Quatermain glanced around, went over to a tree whose long branches hung over the edge of the roof. He took out his knife and quickly cut down two sturdy branches. He unbuttoned his shirt, took it off, stripped off the undershirt and donned the outer one again. He wrapped the white undershirt around the edge of one of the branches.

"Do what I've just done Blaine." Quatermain handed the other branch to his partner. "We will need torches in the darkness of this place. Now… which of us will go first?"

"I will go first," Blaine said, "for I have youth and height on my side."

Quatermain grumbled, half-insulted, but nodded. "Leave the rifle and torch here and I'll pass them down to you."

Blaine put his equipment down, took a deep breath, and lowered himself into the opening. He hit solid ground below and called up, "I'm all right, Quatermain, but I can't see a thing down here! Pass me the torch!"

Quatermain struck a match and lit the shirt at the end of the branch, handed it carefully down to Blaine. As Blaine held the torch, the room in which he had landed was illuminated. The young traveler gasped.

He was in a vast, ancient temple. The ceiling was held up by a series of stone pillars, each of which had been decorated with strange carvings the likes of which Blaine had never seen in person or even in books on history and myth. The entire room was a big circle with strange patterns drawn upon the walls and even on the floor and ceiling. It was at once breathtakingly beautiful and disturbingly strange to see. Blaine was almost mesmerized by the sight.

"Damn it, Blaine, is everything all right down there? I'm waiting!"

"Oh! Quatermain, yes! I'm sorry…this is just…incredible! Hand the rifles and the other torch to me and then lower yourself down. I'll assist you."

Quatermain dropped down into the temple and the two men surveyed the area, torches and rifles in hand. The air inside was colder than it should have been with the jungle sun beating down on the stone roof. The place smelled of age and secrets.

"Have you ever seen such a place in your travels?" Blaine asked.

"Yes," Quatermain said, "there have been things I've stumbled across in Africa that have plainly been there since times forgotten by those men who think they know the history of these lands…but this place, Blaine, is different, perhaps even older. I have seen many things in my years, but this one sets my instincts to ringing out like loud bells at noon! Were it not for the need to find Ben, I would flee this place immediately and never return! But we must find our friend."

"Well he can't possibly be here," Blaine said, "for all I see are these

*"He was in a vast ancient temple."*

curved walls and the hard floor beneath our feet."

"No, Blaine, there is more." Quatermain began to pace the floor, looking much like a beast stalking his prey. "Places like this one are usually more than what they seem to be on the surface. I am beginning to understand why the strange drumming I heard last night seemed so close yet so distant. There is something beneath this temple! The drumming must have come from under the ground! Look around, Blaine, don't just stand there dumbstruck! There must be a way down into the bowels of this ruin!"

"But Quatermain, perhaps we should go back and ask Colonel Huffington for reinforcements. We have no idea what lies beneath this dreadful place."

"Blaine, I no more wish to charge blindly into danger than you do, but Ben may not survive long in whatever sort of place this is if we do not find him! And the same can be said of the nine missing women, assuming they have not yet perished here! We have no choice in the matter, we must press on! Now help me find a way down!"

Blaine began to stalk about the temple in imitation of Quatermain, shining his torch this way and that, checking along the walls and behind the pillars. After some minutes of searching, he called out.

"Quatermain, I've found something over here!"

Quatermain rushed to Blaine's side, peered behind one of the many thick pillars that kept the roof up. In the shadows, the darkness now partly dispelled by firelight, was an opening in the floor, rectangular and large enough for a wide man to fit through. Inside were steps, evenly carved and made of the same ancient stone as the rest of the structure.

"I cannot see how far down into the earth it goes," said Blaine.

"We shall see soon enough," Quatermain said and began to climb into the hole without hesitation. Blaine, admiring the grizzled old hunter's courage, followed.

The steps seemed to go on forever, though Quatermain knew the distance was not as far as it felt, for caution slowed them as they did not trust the cracked and slippery old stone upon which they trod. After what may have been a hundred steps in Quatermain's estimation and a thousand in the mind of Blaine, who was not used to such strange experiences, Quatermain held up a hand to signal that they must pause in their descent.

"Keep your voice down, Blaine, be silent and listen."

"Yes, Quatermain, I hear it too: voices…though I can't make out what they are saying. What shall we do?"

"Continue on, of course, but carefully now. Follow me down slowly. If men are down below, they must be able to see, so they must have light. We shall creep further down these steps and at the first sign of any light ahead of us we must extinguish our torches and make our way to the source of the voices in absolute stealth and silence. We must be ready for anything!"

Several moments and a dozen slippery steps later, Quatermain again gave the signal to stop. Blaine, a step behind and looking over Quatermain's shoulder, could see a pinpoint of light below, at a place where it seemed the long downward climb would finally end. Quatermain pressed the flaming end of his torch hard against the stone wall and twisted it until the fire died. Blaine repeated the action with his own torch. They set the branches down and held their rifles ready, continuing down, even more cautiously as they could no longer see their own feet upon the steps, now navigating only by the little hint of light, like sea captains steering ships by a single lonely star.

Without incident, they reached the bottom of the steps. They stopped just inside the narrow portal that separated the staircase from the room at the end of the descent. Quatermain knelt down and looked in with Blaine standing behind to see over his head. Both men were shocked by what they saw.

There was a vast chamber carved into the earth. In the center was a large fire which gave off a bright light and intense heat. Around the fire stood a series of immense drums which had been the source of the strange music Quatermain had heard in the night. Along the perimeter of the chamber, held in upright positions by heavy chains, stood the nine Englishwomen, captives now, clad only in torn and sparse undergarments, barefoot and with their hair disheveled. Some had apparently dozed off standing while the others stared straight ahead with dazed, stunned, or terrified faces. Nearer to the center, not far from the big drums, was Ben, seated on a stone block and bound by thick ropes that appeared to have been woven together from vines. Some ten feet from Ben's position was a stone table around which sat six men, white men in the tattered remains of clothes of the kind worn by Quatermain and most other Europeans who traveled the jungles of Africa. They were eating and talking, though Quatermain and Blaine could not hear the words from where they hid and watched, for the crackling of the fire was quite loud.

"My god, Quatermain, what manner of place have we discovered? Who are those men and what do they intend to do with the women…and with poor Ben?"

"Judging by their faces," Quatermain answered, "I would guess that they are Dutch. But what their intentions are, I cannot say. I wish I could hear their words from here."

"But if their intentions were friendly ones," Blaine said, "they would not have the women bound to the walls and they certainly would not have killed the native guides so brutally. Why don't we simply shoot them all? With your expert shooting and my fair aim, six targets should not prove too difficult."

"Blaine, don't be foolish! Look closely and you will see that each of those men has a rifle of his own propped against the block upon which he sits. While we may be able to use surprise and shoot down most of them before they can fully react, it is too likely that one or both of us would be struck down as well. We are too outnumbered to act without further consideration."

"Well we cannot sit here and wait forever, Quatermain! What if one of them should come this way and discover us? We must either do something…or flee before doing anything!"

"Shut your mouth, boy, and let me think!" Quatermain sharply snapped.

Blaine kept watching the inhabitants of the chamber. One of the Dutch-looking men stood up now, walked over to where Ben sat bound to the stone block, and slapped poor Ben hard across the face. Ben's head simply rolled from side to side, his eyes half-open, his face bearing the bruises of a brutal beating.

"Damn it, Quatermain," Blaine whispered. "We have to help him."

"Steady, Blaine. Don't do anything stupid."

The Dutchman screamed something in Ben's face, loud enough to be heard over the crackling of the fire and the whimpering noises made by some of the captive women.

"What was that, Quatermain?" Blaine asked. "Is he speaking Dutch?"

"No," said Quatermain, who had at least some familiarity with many languages spoken in Africa, "I have no idea what that was. Whatever he said comes from no tongue of which I have knowledge."

"I don't know what you are saying!" Ben roared back in his tormentor's face. This only made the Dutchman strike him again.

The sight of Ben being hit again angered Blaine and made him clench his fist and tighten his grip on the rifle. Quatermain could hear the younger man's breathing intensify behind him, knew his anger was about to boil over into unwise action.

"Control yourself, Blaine."

Blaine tried. He grasped that rifle as hard as he could, tried to quench the anger with thoughts of anything but the scene that unfolded before his eyes, but like a cracked dam with too much pressure against it, he burst. With a roar of anger, he shoved Quatermain aside and exploded into the spacious chamber. He held his rifle up in front of him and called out, "Leave him alone!"

The Dutchmen all stood at once, raised their guns, but the one who had struck Ben barked out in the strange language and none of them fired. Blaine began to squeeze the trigger, ready to kill whoever his shots hit, but one of the Dutch, moving faster than any normal man can, slammed into him, tackling him, sending the rifle flying from his hand and skidding across the stone floor. Two more rushed over and the three of them grabbed Blaine, hit him a few times to stun him, and proceeded to bind him upon a stone block near to where Ben already sat held fast.

Quatermain, watching the whole event unfold, stood firmly in the doorway, moving back just a bit, enough to let the shadows fully conceal him, knowing that to interfere, to try to rescue Blaine and Ben, would be suicide. The strangers did not appear to want to kill anyone, at least not yet, but it would do no good if Quatermain too were captured.

He saw only one option. It was not a move of cowardice, but one of necessity. Quatermain turned and began to move back up the steps as quickly as he could climb in the dark. He made it up to the point where he felt his foot strike the long branches that he and Blaine had left behind. He lifted one of them, lit it again with a match from his pocket and, now able to see clearly, moved even faster up to the summit of the steps, into the ancient temple above, and managed to scramble out onto the top of the building by getting a good running start, leaping high enough to catch the mouth of the rooftop opening, and hauling himself up and out using every ounce of his strength.

Outside, he lay on the roof for a moment, glad to feel the hot sun beat down on his face, happy to be safe at least for the time being. He listened there for a minute to see if he had been chased, decided he had not, and walked over to the edge of the roof and jumped down to the ground. His landing was a rough one, but Quatermain stood up with nothing worse than a few bruises. He was angry now. He stood there with his fists clenched and thought of Blaine and Ben and those poor young women held by those Dutchmen or whatever they were. He spit on the ground and cursed out loud. He stared at the stone wall of that strange ancient temple and spoke out loud.

"I will return for all of you! You have my oath on that!"

Allan Quatermain started out slowly, steadily. With all his heart he wanted to run, race back to the colony and then get back to the temple with the whole of the British regiment and as many other men as he could muster, but a long, eventful life in Africa had taught him otherwise. One does not, unless it can be helped, he knew, run through the jungle. First of all, there are too many obstacles, too much underbrush, to run safely. Second, the heat will get the best of you if you overexert yourself. Third, the last thing a man wants to do is go rushing past and startling a lion or a cobra or any other predatory beast. Quatermain would keep up a good but careful pace and keep going until forced to rest by hunger or darkness, whichever came first. And once his stomach was full and he was rested and the sun emerged to guide him again, he would continue on. He would not rest, except as needed, until he had reinforcements and had his friends and the missionary women out of the hands of the enemy. That was his plan and he prayed it would not go astray.

As he walked, following the dirt path that led away from the ancient building, Quatermain took stock of his condition. Physically, he was fine. He had plenty of water and had no worries about finding adequate food along the way, for his knowledge of edible plants and about how to catch meat was extensive. He was well armed too: rifle, pistol, and knife. Unless something unforeseen and malignant occurred, he expected no difficulty getting back to the colony. He did have two worries though; would he be given sufficient help by Colonel Huffington when he requested it, and would he be able to make it back into the jungle with that help before it was too late to save Blaine and the others from whatever fate had in store for them? Quatermain kept walking and the questions kept revolving in his mind. How had that temple sat undetected in the jungle for so long? Why had Quatermain never heard of its existence in all his years of intimate familiarity with the region? What strange language was it that the six men who looked Dutch had been speaking? And most importantly, what did they intend to do with their captives?

Everett Blaine opened his eyes. He blinked repeatedly until his vision had adjusted to the strange light of the underground cavern, the dancing flames casting brightness that alternated with the shadows around the edges of the room. Blaine's stomach hurt where he had been punched before being bound to the stone block on which he now sat unable to move. He could turn his head though and glanced to his left and right. Ben was on the next block, head hanging down with chin resting on his chest, unconscious. Along the wall in direct line of Blaine's sight were several of the chained women. The men who had captured him were strolling about the place, ignoring their prisoners, one or another of them occasionally stopping to stoke the big fire or chatter to one of their comrades in the strange language in which they communicated.

Where, Blaine wondered, was Quatermain? Could the old hunter possibly have abandoned his friends? No, Blaine decided, Quatermain would return, hopefully with others. What Blaine had to do then, he knew, was stay alive long enough for help to come. He decided to try to talk to his captors. As one of them walked past, Blaine shouted out.

"Can you understand me? You there, do you speak English? Hello!"

The passerby, a large, stocky man with a blond mustache, paused in front of Blaine, stared for a moment, and went back to walking. Blaine's impatience grew.

"Will one of you men please explain to me what is happening here?"

None of them spoke, but Ben, on his seat not far from Blaine, stirred from his sleep, lifted his head, and talked.

"It is no use, Mr. Blaine! I have tried to talk to them…in English and in the Zulu language and also in the bit of Dutch I know…but they ignore me. In all the hours I have been here, I have not learned what they want with me or with these unfortunate women. Where is Macumazahn?"

"I don't know precisely, Ben, but I hope and pray that he has gone for more men with more guns and will return to free us from this dungeon of horrors! Are your bonds as tight as mine? My legs are tied tight and I cannot work my hands free either!"

"My muscles, Mr. Blaine, are sore from trying, and still these vines will not break. We are trapped until these fiends set us free or help arrives. What can we do but wait?"

"Have you tried to talk to the women, Ben?"

"They do not seem to be able, Blaine. Perhaps they are too frightened by this experience!"

"Well I'm going to try. If these men will not explain our situation to us, perhaps the women, who have been here longer than we, can shed some light on things!"

Blaine turned away from Ben, stared across the chamber at one of the women, a young lady with her eyes open, apparently awake, though with a dazed, horrified expression on her face. He called out to her.

"Hello, Miss, can you understand me? My name is Everett Blaine. I am an American and I wish to understand what is happening here! Can you help me?"

She raised her head a bit, her eyes opened wider, and she coughed as if trying to talk but having difficulty due to thirst.

"It's all right, Miss," Blaine said. "Speak if you can, but do not cause yourself too much discomfort." One of the jailers walked by at that moment and Blaine looked up at him. "Can't you pitiless barbarians see that those women need water? What kind of cruel devils are you?"

Blaine was ignored, but kept talking, his voice getting louder as his frustration escalated. "Listen, you animals: you obviously have no intention of killing us immediately or you'd have done it already…so you don't want us starving or dying of thirst, do you? Those women need water!"

One of the captors did stop in front of Blaine now. He stared down at the bound American and began to speak. The words came out in the strange unidentified language but Blaine suddenly realized that what he was hearing with his ears was not the same as what was going into his mind. Somehow he could understand the message!

*You are correct, young man. Water is necessary for the survival of those we hold here. You will be put to use if you agree to not attempt escape. Will you agree to this?*

Blaine had no idea exactly what was meant by "put to use," but he decided that any change in events was better than being tied to a stone block by a fire.

"I agree."

The Dutchman drew a knife from his belt, quickly cut the vines that held Blaine, then grabbed Blaine's collar and pulled him into a standing position. Blaine stood face to face with his captor, but kept his temper in check despite his desire to strike the man and run for freedom. The Dutchman pointed to an area on the other side of the fire and Blaine followed the gesture with his eyes. There was a large cauldron of water there, with several small tin cups beside it. Apparently, Blaine decided, he was to distribute water to his fellow captives. The words that went into his mind confirmed that.

*Give them enough to make them stay alive…but if you do anything else or try to free them, you will die quickly.*

Blaine nodded and made his way over to the water supply. He picked up one of the cups and dipped it into the pot, filling it with water. He raised the cup to his face, sniffed to be sure the water did not smell rank or polluted. It seemed fresh. He took a small sip, would have smiled at the refreshing coolness had the circumstances been any different. He refilled it and walked over to the first of the women along the wall.

She would have been lovely, Blaine thought, had she not been smeared with dirt, marked with the scratches of being dragged or marched through the jungle with very little clothing to protect her, and forced to stand upright chained to a stone wall, which had the poor girl dancing on the precarious edge between sleep and waking shock that comes from not being able to drop off into full slumber.

"Miss, can you understand me? Can you look at me, Miss? I wish to help you. Can you drink this?"

She opened her eyes halfway, her lips trembling as she came around just enough to see that a man stood before her. Blaine lifted the cup to her lips and gently tipped it to let the water flow into her mouth. She nearly choked but managed to swallow. Blaine let more water flow and she swallowed again. The refreshment seemed to wake her a bit more and she was able to hold her head up and look at Blaine now. Her eyes focused on Blaine and then moved to the left and right to scan the rest of the chamber.

"I…I hoped it might have been a nightmare," she said softly, "but it is all real. Will they kill us…or worse?"

"I don't know," Blaine said, "but please do not give up hope. As long as we are alive, there is a chance we will find a way out of this place. Can you tell me your name?"

"Katherine."

"And I am Everett. Try to keep your hopes up, Katherine. I must go and bring water to your friends now."

Blaine moved along the line that stretched around the chamber walls, bringing water to each of the nine captive women, occasionally going back to the cauldron to refill the cup. All the women drank, some more than others, their conditions ranging from coming awake as much as Katherine to regaining awareness just enough to swallow a bit of the water and stay alive. When he had made his rounds, Blaine brought water to Ben, who had come around enough to drink deeply and utter a strong declaration of thanks. When everyone had drank, Blaine put the cup down by the large pot and stood waiting to see what his captors would do or say next.

Quatermain continued down the dirt path. He walked swiftly but at a measured pace meant to minimize the energy he expended. He kept his senses alert for any signs of danger but so far had seen or heard nothing he would not expect to encounter in the jungle on a warm late morning. Still, he knew in his instincts and his heart that it would not be as easy as strolling back to the colony at a leisurely pace and summoning soldiers to help him retrieve Blaine and the others. Something else would happen; Quatermain would have bet all the possessions he had and everything he would ever own on that.

At noon, with the sun high in the sky, Quatermain stopped. He had to eat. He found shade under a tree at the edge of the path and sat down on the grass. He took two strips of smoked venison from his small reserve of food and munched for a few minutes, washing it down with water from his canteen. Five more minutes, he told himself as he took out his pipe, filled and lit it, and let the smoke relax him. The air was warm and still, noiseless. Quatermain felt the heat on his face and enjoyed the rest, promising himself that he would not waste much time but would rise and be on his way soon. He closed his eyes for a moment and then felt something wrong, his instincts crying out to him, a sudden shift in the thickness of the atmosphere. He heard the twang of a bowstring being released and knew that danger had been sent fast in his direction. Quatermain ducked, fell on his side beneath that tree, felt peril whiz by and heard the impact of the arrow planting itself into the tree that had, only a second before, been behind his head.

He rolled a few feet to one side, sprang up onto his knees, and had his rifle out and aimed in front of his body in an instant. He looked across the path to where the arrow had been shot from. The thick trees obscured his view but behind the green he could hear the sound of men rushing toward him, more than a few he estimated by the sound of the running feet. He expected more arrows, but none flew out of the jungle. He stood, rifle still ready, hoping to shoot down at least some of his attackers before they reached him. But he had to know how many he faced, how heavily they were armed, what sort of men they were. Had they followed him, unheard, from the temple? Were they others of the same sort? Or was this an unrelated attack, hard as that was to believe? All these questions flashed through the mind of Allan Quatermain as danger came closer and closer.

They exploded out from behind the tree line, five of them, the same sort of men who had been in the underground chamber: Dutch-looking, clad

*Quatermain heard the impact of the arrow planting itself into the tree .*

in hunter's attire, armed with rifles, swords, and, in one case, the bow that had interrupted Quatermain's rest.

Quatermain could see murder in their eyes. This was no occasion for talk. He fired his rifle. The one nearest to Quatermain, about to fire his own rifle, was the first to be hit by Quatermain's masterfully aimed shot. The rifle flew off to the side as the Dutchman's chest caved in from the impact of the bullet. As the first attacker died, two of the others fired at Quatermain but missed. Their movements seemed odd to Quatermain, as if they were puppets on strings and not men moving naturally as he was. He knocked one more down with a powerful rifle blast, an instant death shot. Now the other three had come too close. Quatermain stepped back, let the rifle fall to his side, drew his pistol, and took down two more with perfectly placed bullets to the heads. One remained, almost on top of Quatermain's position now, having decided against gunfire and swinging a sword wildly. Quatermain ducked and felt the breeze of the blade passing over his head. When he rose again, his long hunting knife was out and he drove it into the last Dutchman's ribs, twisting it. The final adversary fell on his back, bleeding from a deep wound to the gut. Quatermain was safe, with four foes dead and one dying. He wiped the sweat from his brow, looked around at the carnage he had made, and knelt down beside the still living, but fading enemy.

"Can you understand my words?" Quatermain shouted.

"I can," said the bleeding swordsman, his voice weak but intelligible.

"Why did you try to kill me?"

"We had no choice…we were being controlled…but the spell is broken now and I will die as who I am and not one of their instruments…"

"What do you mean? Whose instruments? Are you from the temple under the earth, like the other men I saw in that pit?"

"Yes…one of the ones below is my brother. The others are…were…my friends…"

"How did you come to be here? What happened to you? Speak quickly man, we haven't much time!"

"We were hunting, exploring. We found the temple and investigated. Most of us did not want to go inside, thought it was just an old ruin…but we felt something, like a strange voice calling us, reaching into our souls to lure us in. I…I do not remember much else. It was as if our minds were elsewhere for a while and our bodies belonged to others. I do not understand what happened. I know little of what occurred before you killed me…but I thank you for letting me die as myself and not one of their slaves…"

Quatermain shook his head. The man who lay before him on the ground was dead and the mystery had only grown stranger. Quatermain strapped his rifle across his back, sheathed his knife, tucked his pistol back into his pants, picked up the dead man's sword which he thought could be useful for hacking his way through any vines and brush that got in his way as he continued his journey, and got back on the dirt path and on his way to the Natal colony.

Was he up against some sort of jungle magic? It would not be the first time he had encountered witchcraft and the work of spirits in the deep jungles. It did not matter much to Allan Quatermain if he faced solid weapons wielded by human warriors or strange magic conjured by sorcery; in either case, his friends and a group of innocent women were being held by evil forces and he felt obligated to help. Onward he went, walking along the path until it ended and the dense green of the jungle resumed. Quatermain kept going, as determined as ever to summon help as soon as possible.

One of the six Dutchmen of the cavern approached Blaine and once again Blaine could hear the sounds coming from his captor's mouth being turned into sense in his mind.

*You did your task well. We will not bind you again, but you must not betray us.*

Thank you," Blaine said. "May I ask questions?" his peaceful cooperation seemed to have worked so far, so he hoped he could progress further in understanding his situation.

*You may ask…but not all will be answered.*

"Who are you?"

*I am one of the six.*

"That is not an answer! Do you have a name?"

*I do not possess a title that you would comprehend.*

"But you're a man, aren't you? You look like one of the Dutch who have come to this part of the world."

*That is the nature of this body, but not of the mind with which you now communicate.*

"I do not understand."

*That is not a question.*

"Well what do you intend to do with us?" Blaine took a different route.

"You have me here, and Ben is bound to that stone and those poor women are chained to your walls! Why do you keep us? What will you do with us?"

*The numbers are almost matched. When that is accomplished, the procedures will commence.*

Blaine's head spun with confusion. He had no idea what those who held him captive were talking about. Had he not been able to distinguish between the sounds coming from their mouths and the words he heard in his mind, he would have assumed he was surrounded by men who had simply gone insane. Perhaps they were insane, he thought, but there had to be more to it than mere lunacy. He needed to know more, to understand what they were talking about, to hear about it in words he could make sense of.

"Listen to me, please," Blaine begged. "Have I not cooperated with you so far? I've helped you, assisted in keeping these women alive! Will you not explain to me precisely who you are, what you intend to do, and what your reasons are? Perhaps I can be of further assistance to you!"

Blaine waited for a moment until the response came, from the mouth of his jailer and also ringing in his head.

*We cannot place full trust in your kind! Just a short time ago, five of our species were slaughtered by one of you not far from this location!*

Species! Blaine wondered what was meant by that. Was the man speaking to him, though he looked human enough, claiming to be some other sort of entity? And who had killed five of them? Was it Quatermain? Blaine suspected so. He needed to keep the dialogue progressing.

"Five of you have died recently? I am very sorry to hear that! How many of you are there?"

*Six remain now…but that number will increase again.*

"I apologize for my ignorance," Blaine said, "but I still do not understand everything. Can you please try to explain fully?"

*Since you have no means of easy escape or resistance…we will provide you with further information.*

Allan Quatermain had decided that the idea of conserving his energy could go to the devil. He had been savagely attacked and had only managed to beat his adversaries by shooting faster and more accurately than they had been able to. He had no idea if more of them were nearby. Also, the dying Dutchman's words had chilled Quatermain to the core. Yes, he had experience battling witchcraft and the mysterious powers possessed by some of the stranger denizens of the jungle, but he did not like those occasions and sincerely hoped this would not prove to be one of them. In either case, he needed help and intended to get it as quickly as he could. He made sure his rifle was securely strapped to his back and began to run. Quatermain was no longer a young man, but his strength was increased by the toughness he had won facing many dangers and always managing to survive even when better men had lost their lives. He could move quickly when he had to and he knew that it was now the time to use all possible speed. Many lives depended upon it.

Everett Blaine felt compelled to return to the stone block upon which he had sat while tied up. He sat down but those who held him in the subterranean chamber did not move to bind him again. He grew relaxed as he sat there, almost on the verge of sleep, feeling a great peace come over his mind and body. When he was calm and no longer afraid, the words inside his mind began again and he listened as the story he had demanded to know was made clear by the voice that did not come from a mouth.

*The information you will now experience comes from minds far older than you realize. We, the souls that have taken residence in these frail flesh shells, have existed as thoughts for many thousands of years, since a time of which none of those who currently examine history are aware. There was a time when this land, the place you now call Africa, was peopled by a civilization that you have no idea ever existed. This stone structure is one of very few places that have survived the ravages of time and still stand in this present age.*

*We were a great people, a proud race who ruled this continent for many millennia, long before the nations that now occupy this place and even before the rise of those you call Egyptians. We raised grand temples and charted the lands and the seas and knew things that still elude the most learned of your kind. But all great civilizations must eventually end and so ours came to its final years. Wars began, dividing our race into factions bent on killing each other. With war and the piling of many corpses comes disease and that too took its toll on our population. Our cities fell and our numbers shrank and our great reign ended in chaos, death, pain!*

*But there were those of us who held out hope that it was not the ultimate, final doom of our kind, for among us were wizards, priests of a great ancient religion who had discovered secrets, ways of controlling the very forces which make life and death what they are. Here in this very chamber, under the temple which still stands above us to this day, rites and ceremonies were carried out that preserved the souls of those willing to give up their bodies and wait for long eons as what you might call ghosts.*

*When a human being is reduced to a mere phantom, it takes many ages for him to regain the strength needed to have any effect at all upon the physical world. It has been a long, long, torturous wait, but now, in this present year, the time has arrived and we, the surviving souls of a lost civilization, are ready to return to the world of solidity and life! Our resurrection has begun!*

Blaine was amazed. He shuddered to think that what he was hearing might be the truth and that he was in fact in the presence of ghosts of some sort, spiritual entities who had taken up residence in the bodies of what had appeared to be ordinary men.

"So you are ancient men who now possess the physical forms of modern men?"

*That is correct, Everett Blaine.*

"And what do you intend to do next? What is the next step in your endeavor?"

*To fully restore our kingdom to the world, we must make more of our kind, new ones to replace those that were lost.*

"How can this happen? I still do not understand?"

*It is quite simple, Everett Blaine. When we became strong enough to take physical forms, we were fortunate that eleven men were hunting in the area near this temple. Eleven of our spirits were able to take control of those bodies. Five of those bodies have been destroyed and the six who are here with you remain. When there were eleven of us, we required eleven women to contain the spirits of our female counterparts and we were again lucky when ten women wandered into the jungle of this region. Unfortunately, we were able to bring only nine of those women here for one was injured when we met them and is thus imperfect and will not be suitable for our purposes. Our solution then would have been to find one more female to make our numbers even, but now the potential women outnumber the men and we will have to adjust the balance yet again. You and your friend, this man you call Ben, shall soon house new, but very old, souls. That will make our number eight! We will then decide whether to look for another woman to host a soul or simply kill one of our captive females to correct the balance.*

Blaine was horrified. "That is barbaric! I will not allow you to steal my body and possess me! And I most certainly will not allow you to do the same to Ben or to murder one of these innocent women or to…to rape them as you intend…both physically and spiritually! The entire idea is intolerable!"

What Blaine heard then was the most terrifying thing yet. Deep in his mind rang laughter, mocking and raucous and supremely confident, followed by more words.

*Do you truly think you can prevent us from carrying out our plans, young foolish man? We have lasted eons in this temple while nations have risen and fallen and risen again. We are immortal souls and we will take what is needed for the restoration of our empire. We shall inhabit flesh again and we shall bring children into this world and we shall conquer!*

Blaine screamed. The horror of the situation was too much for him. He ran past the possessed Dutchmen and past the cauldron of water and past Ben and the captive women and had almost made it to the narrow doorway that led to the stairs when he heard the shot ring out behind him. He expected the pain of a bullet tearing into his back, but that particular agony never came. Instead, he heard the impact of the bullet against the stone ceiling above and felt a piece of loosed rock bounce off his head. The sudden jolt was the last thing he felt as he lost consciousness.

Allan Quatermain could run no longer. He had covered many miles of jungle but had to rest. His legs ached, he was short of breath, and hunger caused great pains in his stomach. He needed food, thought about shooting any sort of small mammal he could find, but decided not to risk the sound of a shot drawing attention to his presence if more men lurked nearby. He decided on a bird instead, managed to knock one out of flight with a well-aimed throw of his knife, and cooked it over a small fire.

After eating, his muscles still sore, Quatermain decided to stay where he was for the night. It was getting dark and he had to rest. He smoked his pipe and selected a spot on the ground, made a pillow of some brush he cut, and laid down to rest. Despite the danger that he suspected might be close, Quatermain drifted away in short time and fell into mostly peaceful sleep, setting the clock in his mind to wake him at first light to resume his trek.

Quatermain was not the sort of man who dreamed very vividly on most nights. A matter-of-fact man, he preferred reality over flights of fancy. On those occasions when dreams did come in bright pageants of images and sounds and events, he knew that something unusual was happening or soon would. As he slept on this night, his mind suddenly felt a presence entering its realm, as if he was not alone in slumber but being watched and even approached by another consciousness, like a spirit was about to visit.

"Is someone there?" Quatermain's dream-self called out in the darkness of his sleeping mind. "Show yourself and reveal your intentions!"

At that instant, as sometimes happens in dreams, Quatermain was no longer surrounded by darkness. He was not in any specific sort of place, but did possess a body that was much like the one he wore in the waking world. Now he stood in the dream-zone and waited for the other presence to reveal itself.

The air seemed to shimmer and shift around Quatermain's dream-self and Everett Blaine suddenly stood before him. It looked very much like the young man Quatermain had come to know and trust in the previous few days, but the vision seemed to blink in and out of existence as if Blaine, or whatever it really was, had to try hard to solidify.

"Blaine! Blaine, is that truly you?"

"You can hear me then, Quatermain?"

"Yes, my boy! And I can see you too! How are you here? Is this not a dream? Are you real or some vision conjured by my sleeping mind?"

"I…believe I am real, Quatermain…but I do not know if I am alive or dead!"

"You are a ghost then, Blaine? I am not certain that I understand!"

"I think, Quatermain, that my spirit has been somehow separated from my body by some terrible magic from long, long ago! I felt myself drifting through a great emptiness, lost in nothing…and then I thought of you and it seems to have brought me to this…this place, wherever I am!"

"This magic, Blaine, is it the work of the men in the chamber below the temple?"

"It is indeed…but they are not only men! It seems that the souls of an ancient people have taken control of the bodies of those Dutch hunters and are now trying to do the same to Ben and to me! Perhaps they have already succeeded, for I can no longer sense my own flesh!"

"Then the man I spoke with in the jungle before he died was telling me the truth, Blaine, for I killed the allies of the cavern-dwellers and one of them, as he lay bleeding, thanked me for setting him free of his possessor! This chain of events is among the strangest things I have experienced in all my years in Africa!"

"I am not ashamed to admit, Quatermain, that I am afraid! I do not wish to die at my young age and already the thought of never again seeing the woman I came to Africa to prove my love for causes me great pain! What can we do?"

"I am not certain what the wisest course of action is, Blaine, but I beg you to tell me everything you know of what is happening! Speak quickly, Blaine, for I must decide what to do!"

Quatermain, still uncertain whether to believe the ethereal figure or dismiss it as a dream brought on by severe exhaustion, listened as the ghost that looked like Everett Blaine related what he claimed to have learned from the inhabitant of the Dutchman's body. Quatermain heard about the long-forgotten civilization and how the souls of those ancient people had waited as ghostly presences in the temple for millennia until they had gained enough strength to take control of the wandering hunters. He listened with horror as Blaine described the spirits' plans to force themselves, in soul and in body, on the captive women to procreate and return their strange race to the earth. Quatermain hoped he was dreaming but feared that it was all true, that Blaine's spirit had indeed been evicted from its mortal shell and sent wandering across the planes between life and death. When the apparition had said its piece, it vanished as if it had never been there at all. Allan Quatermain felt his mind being pulled back to the waking state with great force and he opened his eyes and sat up as the first hints of sunlight appeared on the horizon to begin to chase away the darkness of the African night.

Katherine was crying. Her sobs were loud ones and the tears streamed down her face but she could not wipe them away for her hands were held out at her sides by shackles and chains. She had watched in horror as the strange scene played out before her eyes and she feared she would soon faint from the combination of exhaustion, terror, and desperation.

When the young American man had given her water, Katherine had felt some of her strength and, more importantly, some of her hopes return. But after those few moments of relief, things had turned to the worse again. Blaine had walked over and sat down on the stone block from which he had been released moments before. He had carried on a conversation with one of their captors. It had looked as if information was being relayed to him, but Katherine could not understand the strange language in which it was being spoken. Whatever had been said, it had greatly upset Blaine, for he had tried to flee. He had not gone far, for a shot had been fired, debris had fallen to strike his head, and he had plunged to the ground unconscious.

After the fall, Katherine had watched as the men who held her captive had lifted Blaine from the cavern floor and carried him over to the table where they ate their meals. When Blaine began to stir back to consciousness, three of the Dutchmen had held him down while the others had traced strange shapes in the air with their hands and chanted guttural incantations. The weird ceremony had gone on for a long time, long enough for Katherine to lose any ability to estimate whether it had been minutes or hours or an entire day. Finally, the chanting had stopped, the hands that held Blaine down were withdrawn, and Blaine sat upright on the table. But, even more to Katherine's horror, when he spoke it was not English that came from his lips, but the bizarre language spoken by those who controlled the events in the underground chamber. The poor young American had, it seemed to Katherine from where she observed, had been transformed into one of the monstrous men who held the fates of all the captive women in their hands. That terrible rite completed, they all, Blaine now included, turned their attention to the black man who sat semi-conscious on the other stone block and the process began anew.

Quatermain had no breakfast, only a short sip of water. Willing to waste not a moment, he was up and running at dawn. He was still uncertain if his dreamlike visit with Everett Blaine had been only a sleeping vision or had actually been a ghostly encounter, but it mattered not, for in either case Blaine and Ben, as well as the women, were still in the gravest of danger. Quatermain was determined to make it to the colony by dusk even if he had to use every ounce of strength in his already aching body.

As the sun made its way across the sky and the level of heat rose in the jungle, Quatermain kept moving, pausing only occasionally for a sip of water but never giving in to the urge to rest. Sweat poured from his body and it grew harder and harder to breathe, the screaming of his muscles reminding him that he was no longer a young man, but the running went on, his footsteps flattening many small plants, his knees bending as he occasionally leaped clear over a rock or shrub, hoping with each jump that the landing would not cause a bad turn of the ankle. On and on he ran like a man chased by a hungry lion. At one point, he found himself thinking that perhaps a hungry lion on his tail would indeed be of some help, for it would give him even more incentive to speed along toward his destination.

By midday, Quatermain reached the place where the jungle ended and the grassy plain began. He rushed out into the open, the sun beating down even hotter on his head, and hurried across the field. His head was spinning now, his chest pounding with each breath. The further he went, the closer the exhaustion he now felt came to crushing him in both body and soul. His head throbbed and his sight grew hazy. He began to feel sick. He knew he had pushed himself past the boundary of sense and his body could take no more. His footsteps grew clumsy and uneven, he nearly stumbled several times. Nearing collapse, he saw, not terribly far away, a wagon drawn by horses and carrying a uniformed two-man British patrol. He stopped running, gathered all his remaining strength for one last waking act, took a deep breath and cried out, "Over here! The need is desperate!" and collapsed on the hot, brown and green ground.

Katherine did not know how long she had been asleep this time. Her eyes opened and she lifted her head as much as her chains and her weakened state would allow. The fire in the center of the room was still ablaze and she could see the same complement of people who had been there before. Her eight remaining friends were still chained in their positions around the edges of the room, some in worse conditions than others. In the middle of the chamber stood the six Dutchmen and the two new men, the American and the African, both of whom now wore facial expressions that matched those of the original six men. They all looked at each other as if a conversation was taking place, but no lips moved and no audible words were uttered. Hands gestured though and heads nodded. After what looked like a long period of debate, the group of men dispersed and its members began to walk separately about the chamber, pacing back and forth, glancing at each of the female prisoners, Katherine included, like customers in a butcher shop selecting pieces of meat for supper. Katherine felt ice flow through her veins and indescribable fears fill her heart.

She watched as the tallest of the men walked over to the spot where Margaret Edwards, the woman who had led the others on their crusade into the jungle, was chained to the wall. The tall man stopped and looked at Margaret's barely covered body, his head moving up and down like that of an art critic appraising a sculpture, and finally let out a word that was gibberish to Katherine's ears. She watched as the other men went through

*He took a deep breath and cried out, "Over here! The need is desperate!"*

similar motions, each appearing to select a woman. Emily was chosen, then Anne, and so forth until most were accounted for. Everett Blaine, or his body at least, for he no longer seemed to be driven by the same soul, stopped in front of Katherine, reached out, stroked her hair for an instant, then uttered what Katherine thought was the same word that the tall man had said.

Within minutes, each of the eight men stood before one of the women. Katherine looked past Blaine, glanced back and forth across the room, and saw that only Julia did not have one of their captors near her. Katherine watched as the man who seemed to have chosen Margaret stepped away from his woman and approached Julia. She guessed what was about to happen and was terrified that she might be correct. She wanted to close her eyes, not see anything more, but her eyelids were paralyzed open, so frozen with fear was her entire expression. The tall man walked up to Julia, grabbed her by the face, one large hand on each delicate cheek, and violently twisted her neck. The snap was loud, horrific. Julia did not cry out, for there was no time for that; her head slumped forward, chin resting on breastbone, and she moved no more. Katherine whimpered at the sight and several of the other women, those who were conscious enough to be somewhat aware of circumstances, screamed.

As Katherine's body shook with the horror of what had just happened, part of her mind could not help wondering if Julia was the lucky one.

Allan Quatermain sat straight up in bed and cried out, "Where the devil am I? Is anybody here?"

The question was instinctive, a natural reaction to waking up in a state of confusion, but he knew almost instantly where he was. He knew a barracks when he saw one. He then recalled that the last thing he had seen had been the wagon driven by soldiers on patrol around the perimeter of the colony. They must, he knew, have picked him up and brought him back with them. He felt tired, sore. He was fully dressed, even still in his boots. He had no idea how long he had been asleep, but saw the light of day through the window. Was it, he wondered, not yet night or had he lost an entire evening and morning to exhaustion?

He got out of bed, looked around the room, most of it filled by empty bunks belonging to soldiers who were now up and about on duty. He found his rifle, pistol, knife, and canteen on a small storage chest at the foot of the bed. He gathered his things and walked out into the hallway of the sturdy wood building. A sentry waited outside the door.

"What time is it, soldier?" Quatermain demanded.

"I have no watch, sir," the young man, who looked barely old enough to shave once a week, said, "but I'd guess it to be just short of noon."

"Blazes," Quatermain muttered. "Where is Colonel Huffington?"

"The colonel is in his office, sir, with orders to not be disturbed for several hours. He had many important…"

Quatermain shoved his way past the startled sentry and stormed down the halls of the barracks. He had spent much time among the British soldiers stationed at the colony and knew his way well. He ignored the raised hand of the sergeant at the colonel's door and barged his way in.

"Importance my eye," Quatermain snapped as he halted in front of Huffington's desk to find the colonel with his head down, asleep on a pile of papers, a foghorn snore echoing through the room's air.

Quatermain gave the front of the desk a sharp kick with his heavy boot, sending tremors through the wood and causing the startled officer to sit up with a roar and a confused look while the sergeant, who had followed Quatermain in, bellowed, "Sorry, sir, I tried to stop him!"

"Colonel, this is not time for rest! I must have men and guns immediately!"

"Sit down, Mr. Quatermain! I'll give you nothing without a proper explanation of why you were running across the plain until you collapsed, of what has become of Mr. Blaine and that orderly you took with you, and of just why you so desperately need *my* men and *my* guns. Now sit down!"

Quatermain wanted to sit, still feeling the effects of his long foolhardy run through so many miles of jungle, but he resisted temptation, preferring to face the colonel on his feet and adamantly make his argument.

"They are not your guns and men, Colonel! The army belongs to the British people and there are nine British women in very great danger out there in that jungle along with my American friend and Ben the orderly! It is your duty and obligation, sir, to offer assistance to those of Her Majesty's subjects who require it!"

"And of what, exactly, Quatermain, does this great danger consist? What…or who is threatening the lives of the women and Mr. Blaine?"

"Dutchmen, sir," Quatermain said, deciding to water down the strange truth to keep the colonel from locking him up on suspicion of drunkenness or insanity. "But something is wrong with these Dutch! They are suffering from some form of jungle-born lunacy, perhaps brought on by fever or the consumption of some berry that ought not to have been eaten. Whatever the cause, sir, these Dutchmen have become violent, seem to have killed the missionaries' guides and that poor girl who escaped, and they now hold the remaining women and my two companions in a ruined temple more than a day's trek from here."

"I see," said Huffington, scratching at his mustache. "And how many of these Dutch are there?"

"At least six are still alive, Colonel. There were five more, but I killed them."

"Quatermain…the sergeant here will take you to have some food. Return here in one hour and I will inform you of my decision in this matter."

Quatermain stomped out with the sergeant just behind him. He did not want to wait an hour, for he was worried about Blaine and Ben, but he saw no choice. Better to go along with the colonel's request and hope that his plea for help would be taken seriously. Also, he knew, the food would help him regain his strength for the journey back into the jungle, alone or with reinforcements.

Everett Blaine was lost in a sea of darkness and fear. He saw nothing, felt nothing, but was conscious on some level between the physical and spiritual. He did not know if he was alive or dead, as if he had left his body but his soul was not yet allowed to cross the barrier into the afterlife, if there was indeed such a place. He thought he had seen Quatermain, spoken to him in a dreamlike atmosphere, but could not be certain if that had been real or part of the hallucinations of a dying spirit. If he remained in limbo for long, Blaine feared, he might go insane beyond repair.

Katherine had passed out at some point after witnessing the fate of Julia. Now she came back to consciousness to find Everett Blaine's body standing before her again, his facial expression no longer matching what it had been when Blaine had given her water many hours earlier. Around the room, similar scenes took place as each of the men had returned to their chosen women and were unlocking the shackles that had held them to the wall for so many terrible hours.

The chains loosed, Katherine stumbled forward with her feet numb from lack of motion, and fell into Blaine's arms. Disgusted by his touch, which felt cold and lizard-like now, she tried to push him away. She screamed, slapped him, and fell backwards onto the hard stone floor. The body of Blaine spoke, the strange language coming out and making no sense to Katherine, but words rang in her mind as if her brain was, through some magic, translating his sounds into English.

*Do not struggle. You must eat, as all human beings must. You cannot be allowed to die, for we have uses for you and the others.*

As he spoke, Katherine saw that the table in the center of the chamber was now heaping with food: cooked meats, fruits from jungle trees, jugs of drink. The men must have gone hunting and gathering while the women had been asleep, she realized.

Instinct took over her mind, made her aware that she did not want to die, not while any hope of freedom was left in her heart. She struggled to stand, felt sensation returning to her limbs, allowed Blaine to guide her to the table where others were gathering now. She ate and drank, mechanically and without enjoyment, for the fear was almost too much to bear, but she felt life returning to her and strength coming back. Perhaps, she thought, there was still a chance of surviving the ordeal.

❀ ❀ ❀

"Quatermain," Colonel Huffington said, "based on your estimation of the problem out there in that jungle, how many men do you want?"

"To be sure we're a strong enough force, Colonel, I want at least a dozen troops, plus men to carry equipment, for we're going to need blankets and medical supplies and we don't want to overburden each man because we must move quickly if we're to have a chance of saving the captives."

"You ask for a lot, Quatermain."

"I ask for a chance to save the lives of innocents!"

"All right, Quatermain...I'll allow this affair to go forward. Sergeant Drake here will assemble the men and supplies and lead them, under your guidance of course."

Drake, a barrel-chested sergeant with a walrus mustache, snapped a salute and barked, "I'll have it all ready to go in half an hour's time, sir!"

Quatermain followed the sergeant out to oversee the preparations and was soon happy to see that Drake was no coward like the first sergeant to go into the jungle with Quatermain had been. Brant had turned and retreated when things had gone gruesome, but Drake was the sort of soldier Quatermain had always respected. There he stood, like a uniformed god in the middle of the field, his thunderous voice blasting out orders as privates and corporals ran about assembling the guns and supplies needed for the adventure on which they were about to embark. Soon enough, in just the amount of time the sergeant had promised, the caravan was ready to leave.

Quatermain would lead, with Sergeant Drake at his side. Behind them would be six soldiers followed by six natives to carry supplies with the other six troops at the rear of the line so that the contingent was covered on both ends in case of attack. Drake had been sure to select men who were strong, healthy, and well-rested so that they could travel as fast as possible on foot through the jungle.

As soon as they were all lined up, Quatermain and Drake took their places at the head of the formation. Private Chadwick, the man on the left in the line just behind the sergeant, blew a mighty note on his trumpet to signal the squad to move and twenty-eight sturdy boots and twelve Zulu sandals began to flatten the grass on the plain between the barracks and the jungle. Help was on its way to Blaine and the others. Allan Quatermain hoped and prayed that it would not be too late.

Everett Blaine, bodiless and lost, tried to keep something resembling rationality. Every time his mind began to spin and the panic grew worse, he forced himself to calm down enough to think. All was dark, not like the night when no stars shone down, but like the total absence of any light at all, like what Blaine imagined blindness to be like. The difference was that a blind man has eyes that do not function. In his ethereal state, Blaine had no eyes or ears or flesh or bones at all. If he had ever felt any sensation comparable, it had been when he was a boy of eight and had almost drowned. As he thought back to that terrifying experience, he recalled how he had managed to survive it. Lost in water, feeling nothing above or below his thrashing body, he had gathered all his will and pushed mightily with all his limbs, propelling himself up with as much force as he could muster until his head broke the waterline and he found salvation and air.

He had no body with which to push now, but he had to try something, anything to find his way back to the world. He could stand the in-between no longer. He thought of all he was on the verge of losing. He thought of Gloria Holloway and how beautiful she was and how he wanted to make her his wife. He thought of his home in Atlanta and his father and mother. He thought of poor Katherine, still a prisoner of the possessed Dutchmen. He remembered Ben, the jolly, loyal hospital orderly who had bravely marched into the jungle alongside Allan Quatermain and the soldiers. He thought of all he had to lose if he let his soul be forever separated from his body by the foul machinations of the men in the underground chamber. When his anger and his pain and his desperation reached a point where it could grow no stronger, Everett Blaine pushed his spirit as hard and fast as he could and he flew through the void.

The soldiers, led by Quatermain and marching under the command of the stern Sergeant Drake, marched quickly and efficiently. They made excellent time crossing the grassy plain and were soon deep in the jungle. They reached the place where the six native guides had been slaughtered and kept on going even if some of the younger men turned pale at the sight of all the wrecked corpses. They passed the place where the clothing of the female missionaries had been discarded and the sight of such wretched treatment of women made them march faster, even more determined to accomplish their mission. Quatermain was happy to have, this time, a group of stalwart men with him, men who wanted to do what they had been dispatched to do, with no interest in running back to the safety of the colony without seeing the quest through.

When they had made it more than half the way to the ruined temple, the rapid march halted and the troops formed a circle and sat down. Sacks of rations were opened and the contingent ate and rested. Those who smoked broke out their pipes and relaxed. Others talked amongst themselves, the soldiers in English and the load carriers in Zulu. Quatermain and Sergeant Drake sat together and compared knowledge of the zone of jungle into which the trek had taken them.

"I've often wondered," Drake said, "why the native population never seemed to hunt this region more than they do. Perhaps they know, on some plane of the mind that they are not even fully aware of, that this section holds danger. From what you said in the colonel's office, Quatermain, those Dutch you encountered have truly gone wrong in the mind! Do you really think such a change is the result of something as simple as fever or the eating of bad berries?"

"I see, Drake," Quatermain answered, "that you were wise enough to perceive that I told Colonel Huffington less than the entire truth. I did so only because I know that he lacks the experience to fully realize the strangeness that one may encounter out here in the thick green world. Yes, Drake, there is more to it than mere poisoning by fruit or fever, though I do not fully understand what did happen. One of the Dutchmen I killed lived long enough to tell me that he had, in his words, been controlled or possessed by some sort of spirit. Judging by what I saw in the chamber beneath the temple, all of his fellows suffered the same fate! And then, Drake, as I slept out of necessity on my journey back to the colony to summon help, I had a dream of a kind I have never had before. In my sleeping state, Everett Blaine, the young American came to me and told me that his soul had been cast from his mortal shell and wandered now, for his place in his body had been taken by a spirit of great antiquity! Blaine told me of the terrible plans these ghostly minds have for the poor captive women. As weird as all that must sound to you, Sergeant, what choice do I have but to believe the words of that familiar apparition after all I had already witnessed on my first trip to this area?"

"That is quite a tale, Quatermain," Drake laughed, but the chuckle was tempered with dread. "Whether what has occurred is truly as strange as you say, I do not know, but it changes nothing about the fact that women are endangered by those crazed Dutch, and for that reason we must continue our journey."

With that, Drake stood up and let out a roar of the sort that can only come from the throat of a sergeant of the best kind. "Get on your feet, men! You've sat and smoked long enough! It's time to march!"

When the food on the table had all been consumed, the eight women were lined up and forced to march up the long, narrow set of stone steps that led up out of the chamber and into the temple above. Four of the male captors led the way, lighting the staircase with torches, and four followed behind the women, all of them bearing rifles and some also possessing swords or knives. Katherine was in the middle of the line, between Emily and Anne, both of whom occasionally let out a whimper or a sob. The climb was difficult. The steps were cold and hard, jagged in a few places. Soft feet, unaccustomed to walking shoeless, did not fare well on such a surface and some of the women stumbled once or twice or nearly twisted an ankle, but they fought on, afraid of what might be done to them if they did not proceed.

Soon, they were at the top and inside the temple. One of the captors walked over to a section of the curved stone wall and pressed on the hard carvings. A second later, the wall opened, a thick panel hinging out enough to let the jungle's light and heat come streaming in, revealing a door wide enough to allow any one of the sixteen to pass through easily. Like captive cattle, the eight women were herded out into the open. For an instant, Katherine thought of running away, darting into the jungle and hoping her friends would follow, but she thought of the rifles and decided against it. She knew little about surviving in such an environment, especially barely clothed, barefoot, and lost. She mentally cursed her own stupidity for embarking on the silly crusade to begin with. Part of her mind tried to hold on to hope, tried to remember how to pray. The other half wished she had been the one who had been left alone when the men had selected their women. Wherever Julia's soul had departed to, it had to be better than wherever they were being led now.

Quatermain and his party marched on until dusk began to bring its curtain down over the world. When darkness began to block their way, Sergeant Drake called out for the company to halt and camp was hurriedly but efficiently set up. Food was distributed again and Sergeant Drake even washed down his supper with a hearty mouthful of whiskey he had brought with him, offering some to Quatermain, who declined. The lesser-ranked men though were forbidden to imbibe while on duty and would not be considered off-duty until the task assigned them was complete.

When all were full, the men entered their tents and fell asleep. Two guards would stand watch at all times, one soldier and one Zulu, working in shifts. Quatermain was the only man other than the sergeant granted the luxury of his own private tent, but he had no plans to make much use it that night. While the others rested, Quatermain prowled the perimeter of the camp, true to the name give him by the natives: Watcher-by-night.

A small fire still glowed in the middle of the encampment, casting its light wide enough that Quatermain was able to see a good way into the surrounding jungle. He listened too, his sharp sense of hearing penetrating the thickness of the jungle, searching for any hint of human—even altered human—activity. There was nothing. All through the night he watched and waited, refusing to let his guard down even as the shifts of assigned sentries changed and men who had less stamina than Quatermain got their rations of rest.

Night had fallen by the time the sixteen walkers finally stopped. They women were ordered to lie down on the jungle floor and sleep. They rested, having no choice but to obey, but few of them managed any true sleep. When the morning light came, they rose again, walked a while more, and finally reached their destination.

A clearing had opened in the jungle to reveal a pond, round and perhaps thirty feet across. The water was calm and encircled by a thin strip of sand. Trees hung out over the water and jungle birds of many colors flew overhead, occasionally swooping down to fill their beaks with the cool water. It occurred to Katherine that it would have been a splendid scene, fit for a painting perhaps, if not for the awful circumstances that had led to her discovering it. So exhausted was she when they stopped, that she fell onto her knees on the sand, relieved beyond measure to no longer force her feet, which were scratched and bleeding from the jungle's floor, to bear all her weight. But no sooner had she fallen down than Everett Blaine's strong hands made her rise again. Cruelly and with no shame on his face, Blaine tore the few remaining shreds of clothing from Katherine's body, leaving her standing there naked and horrified. Around the pond, the other seven men did the same to the other seven women. Shrieks of embarrassment and fear echoed above the little lagoon.

When all that was done, the voices of the men sounded in their strange language and once again the women heard it in their minds in a way that could be understood despite the differences in the words.

*Enter the water and cleanse yourselves, for you must make pure vessels for your new souls.*

A few of the women backed away from the edge of the water and were promptly pushed forward again by the closest males to their positions. Hesitantly but surely, each woman moved forward, dipped a toe and then slowly walked further in until all were neck high in the pond.

As they stood in the water, which felt refreshing even with such fear haunting all their thoughts, Katherine looked at the men who stood upon the shore. Strangely, she realized, their faces betrayed no lust, as if what they were doing was simply duty in preparation for some great purpose which must proceed without obstacle. Katherine plunged her head beneath the surface of the water, soaking her hair. When she broke the surface again and looked over at the man who had once been called Everett, she saw that his eyes had closed, his face was wrinkled in something that may have been pain or fear or some other discomfort. She stared.

*Blaine tore the few remaining shreds of clothing from Katherine's body.*

Everett Blaine felt like his mind had been hurled through infinity by a catapult of cosmic proportions. He had pushed with a great thrust of will and felt as if he were flying, though he had no body. Then, abruptly, the sudden journey ended with a jolt like hitting a wall, but not painful at all since no nerves connected any physical awareness to his mind. His mental eyes scanned his surroundings and he began to understand.

He had a body again, but it seemed to be a thing of light, much like when he had seen Allan Quatermain in what he supposed was Quatermain's dream. The room he stood in now was round like the ruined temple. Across from him, he was shocked to see, stood a figure! The man was powerfully muscled and had the dark skin of a native African, but his features were different than a Zulu like Ben, perhaps with a hint of the shape one might see in the face of a man from Japan. The two men in the round chamber stood and stared at each other for what seemed like forever. Blaine knew where they were: he now stood in his own mind, in the ethereal place that keeps a man's soul connected to his body. The man who stood before him, he suddenly realized, was the usurper, the one who had evicted him from his own flesh and bone home and sent his spirit spiraling out into the nothingness beyond.

"You do not belong here!" said the usurper. This time Blaine understood his words even when uttered vocally. Why would he not understand? It was *his* mind in which the message was said.

"Your arrogance disgusts me!" Blaine shouted. "This mind is mine, as is the body to which it is tied. I was born to it and it is the vessel of my life! You are the one who must leave. Get out!"

With those words, Everett Blaine charged, absolute rage in his expression, hands raised with the intent to batter the intruder senseless and perhaps even to death, if a man who was already a ghost could be slain again.

They collided, two souls in one mind fighting for control of one body. As soon as they met in violence, Everett Blaine knew that he now had the advantage. He was angrier, driven by rage and fear and desperation while his opponent clearly had not expected him to return and fight. Blaine hit him again and again and again. There was no blood, no breaking of bone, for the ethereal bodies were composed of different stuff than fleshly ones. But the usurper began to crumble under Blaine's fists and finally, with a long, weak whimper of loss and pain, the intruder faded away. Blaine stood there for a moment and then he opened his own eyes, the ones in his material head, and saw daylight again the way men are meant to see it.

He looked out over the pond, saw the eight naked women in the water, a sight that would have thrilled him had the circumstances been any different, but now it horrified him for he knew that it was all part of the process of turning living beings into things that should no longer exist. His eyes focused on one woman in particular and he called out her name.

"Katherine!"

Katherine saw Everett Blaine open his eyes; she saw his entire expression change, as if the pain she had seen an instant earlier had subsided. He looked, she thought, like himself again, like the gentle young man who had brought water to her at the time when thirst had nearly stolen her last ounce of strength. Was it possible that he had somehow returned from the place his soul had been banished to?

She was stunned when he called out her name. She saw the other men around the pond all turn and look at him as if shocked that he had called to her. She saw him turn and run and she knew she had to follow, that he was her only chance at escaping captivity. She moved through the water, made it onto the circle of sand that surrounded the pond, forced modesty from her mind, and ran naked into the surrounding jungle, following the only man for perhaps many miles around in whom she had any faith at all.

Quatermain and the others were on the march at first light, in the same formation, with the same urgency. They soon reached the beginning of the strange dirt road that Quatermain knew would lead them to the temple which represented the center of the strange events that had brought them into the jungle.

The road made things easier and the journey sped up. No longer having to worry about tripping on vines, stepping over chunks of rock, or avoiding slithering snakes, the men marched swiftly on, passing miles of ground, travelling closer and closer to their destination. Quatermain and Drake told everyone to stay alert and keep their eyes and ears open for danger, for those they pursued might be out of the temple and roaming the area.

Katherine caught up to Blaine. The two of them hid behind a small hill in the jungle a mile from the small pond. There had been some sounds of chasing behind them but the others had seemed to have either stopped their hunt or veered off in the wrong direction. Perhaps, Blaine thought, they had stopped because their numbers were still evenly divided between male and female even with him and Katherine having fled. That balance between the genders seemed to be essential to their plan, based on what Blaine knew of the situation.

When they stopped, Blaine saw that the poor frightened girl was ashamed of her nakedness, her hands held up over her body to cover her breasts. He stripped off his shirt, gave it to her, and she put it on. She trembled.

"We are safe…at least for now," Blaine said. "Try to be calm. I need your help."

"What can I do?"

"I was not conscious, not in control of my own body when the temple was left behind," Blaine explained. "I do not know the path we took to arrive at that pond, but we must go back to the temple, for I suspect that Allan Quatermain, the man with whom I came on this journey, will return to try to help us. Do you remember the route you travelled?"

Katherine looked back in the direction from which they had run. She tried to visualize the way she had travelled on the forced exodus from the temple.

"I think…though I cannot be sure…that it is that way." She pointed.

"A good guess," Blaine said, "is better than complete uncertainty. We must walk then, but quietly, for we do not know where the others are."

"I will try to keep up," Katherine promised, beginning to limp along slowly beside Blaine, her legs tired from running, feet battered from the flight from the pond.

"We will both do our best," Blaine assured her, "and hope it is enough."

Blaine and Katherine were indeed travelling in the right direction. They found the fourteen others, the seven men leading their seven naked captive women back through the jungle, back in the direction of the temple. Blaine decided that the best way to proceed would be to keep a parallel course to the others, staying silent and stepping lightly to avoid notice. Once they reached the temple area, he and Katherine would follow the dirt path back toward the jungle and hope to find Quatermain along the way. He could think of no other plan. He hoped Katherine would be strong enough to make the journey.

The trip was a fast one now as the men forced the women to keep going, trudging over jungle ground despite their occasional stumbles or cries for rest. The parade of fear kept moving as Blaine and Katherine shadowed. By the time the sun reached its greatest height at noon, the temple had been reached. The stone door at the rear of the building opened after the man who had once been Ben manipulated it by some means known to no man born in the nineteenth century. The fourteen disappeared inside and the secret door shut behind them.

Once he was sure they would be unseen, Blaine took hold of Katherine's hand and led her around the perimeter of the large round temple and onto the dirt path at the front. They walked faster now; they were almost joyful at being sure they could no longer be seen by those who had kept them in chains. But the happiness was tempered by the thought of the remaining women still being trapped. They went on, hoping to find help before it was too late.

Their hopes were soon rewarded, for only ten minutes after they began along the dirt road, Allan Quatermain marched into sight accompanied by a dozen armed soldiers and a handful of Zulus. Everett Blaine had to blink hard to hold back tears of relief.

"Blaine, my boy, you've managed to get away from those Dutch bastards!"

Blaine fell to his knees in front of Quatermain, exhausted. Katherine fell to the ground beside him, even worse off, almost unconscious.

Quatermain turned to Drake. "Sergeant, blankets to cover this poor girl, food and water for Mr. Blaine! Tell your men to make it quick!"

The entire party halted there, set up a very temporary camp. Blaine wolfed down his food and felt his strength returning. Katherine had been taken aside for examination by one of the corporals, a man with medical training. As Blaine replenished himself, Quatermain and Sergeant Drake sat beside him.

"There are seven men inside," Blaine explained, "including poor Ben, who has become one of them! Seven women remain too, held prisoner. They killed one of them to even their numbers, the bloody animals! All the men are armed."

Quatermain spoke next, already deciding on a course of action.

"Sergeant, we will leave three of your men here, the medical man and two others, as well as the natives. They will watch over the young lady. Blaine, you must stay here and rest."

"I will not," Blaine argued. "Those monsters tried to steal my life. I owe them for that!"

"If you must come along, Blaine," Quatermain nodded in understanding, "I will not prevent it. Do you remember where we hid Ben's rifle?"

"I do."

"Then retrieve it and make it yours when we get there. Sergeant, you and the other nine of your men will come with me. Our goal is to save the women and, if possible, the Zulu who is with them, for he is a friend and a good man when not possessed by spirits of a lost race! As for the formerly Dutch, I fear they may be too long possessed and beyond salvation. If we must kill them, then that is how it shall be. We must waste no time."

With Quatermain at the lead and Everett Blaine just behind him, twelve men went forth to face the enemy.

※ ※ ※

As they came within sight of the temple, Drake signaled for the men to stop. It was the most fortunate signal he had ever given, for a shot rang out and a bullet struck the ground mere inches in front of the sergeant.

"We're being fired upon!" one of the men cried out.

"Move back, all of you," Quatermain said.

The company split into two sides, ducking into the jungle on either side of the dirt path, taking cover behind trees and looking out and up at the source of the shot. Quatermain, Blaine, Drake, and three of the soldiers were on the right side while the other six troops had taken the left.

"Quatermain, it is Ben up there shooting at us!"

Ben stood atop the temple, rifle aimed down at the ground, preparing to fire again, but before he could take proper aim, a shot rang out from the opposite side. The bullet struck, Ben's white shirt blossomed with red, and he fell forward off the roof and struck the ground with a terrible sound and did not move again.

"Damn it!" Quatermain spat. "All of you hold your fire!"

But fire was not held, for the ends of five more rifles appeared on the roof, though the shooters were now prone, which made for excellent protection. They all fired at once, not very skillfully, for no one on the ground was hit, but it was sufficient to keep the soldiers from advancing. Round after round was exchanged, with men alternating between firing and ducking behind trees. Dozens, perhaps hundreds, of bullets were wasted as the confrontation became a stalemate.

"Quatermain," Blaine shouted over the thunder of guns, "what can we do? This will go on until all the ammunition is spent!"

"History will consider me a fool if this stupid act puts an end to me," Quatermain said, "but perhaps I can tip the scales in our favor. Stay here!"

With that, Quatermain turned and ran back into the jungle, opposite the direction of the temple. Blaine watched him go, wondering what the tough old hunter was thinking.

Long years of practice had taught Allan Quatermain to accurately predict the path a bullet would take once put into flight. It was that skill that made him such a good shot and that skill that he put to use now in a different way. Quatermain ran into the jungle and in a large loop that took him away from the temple and then back toward it, bringing him to a point along its side where he knew he would be safe from the crossfire produced by the exchange of shots between the British troops and the men who had once been Dutch. Once his position had been selected, he chose a tree and climbed, settling onto a perch some twenty feet above the ground. From up there he could see clearly onto the roof of the temple where the five shooters lay sending round after round at the soldiers below. Five of them up there, Quatermain knew, meant that one had remained beneath the temple to keep watch over the captive women. Now Quatermain raised his rifle, steadying his body in the tree to keep the recoil of his shots from knocking him out of the branches to a bone-breaking fall to the jungle floor. He took aim.

The first three shooters on the roof never knew what happened. Three quick shots from off to the side of the temple and three ancient souls were sent spiraling back to darkness, the bodies they had occupied struck by bullets fired with such perfect accuracy that death was immediate. The other two stopped firing at the soldiers on the ground, turned about, determined where the new attack had originated, and began sending shot after shot into the trees.

Quatermain winced as a bullet crashed into the branch next to the one on which he sat, missing him by a mere two inches, sending splinters flying and leaves fluttering down to the earth. He had to get down. He dropped his rifle first, hoping it would sustain no damage. He brought himself down next, scurrying squirrel-like down the trunk, picked up his rifle, and ran back toward the others. He hoped he had evened the odds enough to be of help.

It was Sergeant Drake who realized the difference first.

"What's happening? They're firing in the wrong direction!"

"It must be Quatermain," Everett Blaine shouted.

"You and you," Drake said, turning to his men, "advance, quickly but cautiously. The rest of you," he raised his voice now so all his men could hear, "keep firing, but aim high so you don't hit your own!"

The two soldiers ran forward, out of cover and toward the wall of the temple. They reached it as the bullets of their comrades flew over their heads and the shots of the men atop the roof continued to ring out. At the wall, they looked back at Sergeant Drake, who know signaled them to go up. The shorter but thicker of the two soldiers held out his hands, fingers intertwined and palms up, and boosted his partner up. As the taller of the two young men pulled his body up onto the roof, he saw that the two men atop the building were still firing off into the trees. Their backs were turned. Thrilled with his luck, the young private stepped onto the roof, fired his rifle twice at a range from which only the poorest shot could miss, and saw the shattered bodies of his first two kills crumple.

"They're down!" he shouted, waving his arms victoriously. "It's all clear!"

Quatermain had run back through the surrounding jungle and now rejoined the others. Sergeant Drake led the company up to the wall of the temple, chose four men to stand guard on the ground, and ordered the others up onto the roof.

"One of them remains inside, I believe," said Quatermain. He stood with Blaine and Drake as they looked down into the rooftop opening. Behind them, soldiers were lowering the bodies of the five dead Dutchmen down to the men on the ground. They dead would be buried properly, regardless of what spirits had possessed them at the end.

"I will go down first," Sergeant Drake bravely volunteered.

"No," said Quatermain, "for I was the man originally hired for the task of retrieving the missing women. This series of events is my responsibility and so I must be the first to climb down into danger's jaws."

"And I," Blaine insisted, "will be with you as I have tried to be since this matter began!"

Torches were made and lit and Quatermain, Blaine, and Drake descended into the temple, finding nothing of importance on the ground level. It was empty, just an old room of strong pillars and strange carvings. They made their way to the stairs and began the journey into the earth.

Quatermain ran down quickly as if he had memorized the placement of the steps and where any perilous points might cause him to stumble. Blaine and Drake proceeded more slowly, carefully. Quatermain reached the bottom first and, wasting no time, burst into the subterranean chamber.

He tossed his torch aside, for the chamber was lit by fire as it had been on his last visit. The seven women were sitting along the curved wall, not chained, but held there by fear of the rifle their one remaining captor had aimed at them.

The last survivor of the risen ancient souls turned to face his new visitor. He stared at Quatermain, hatred burning in his eyes, and began to speak.

Suddenly, unexpectedly, Quatermain heard words inside his head. The sounds coming from his foe's mouth were nonsense, but the message reaching Quatermain's mind was plain, clear English.

*We had almost risen again to rule this world. The things we would have done...the temples we would have raised...the miracles we would have shown you all...the nations we would have conquered...*

The words were meant to distract, Quatermain knew, but while his mind was busy listening to the bragging of a last, desperate ghost-man, his eyes were watching the hands. The instant the finger on the trigger began to squeeze, Quatermain fired his own rifle. The shot slammed into the chest, exploded out the back, struck the wall behind the falling body, and clattered to its place of rest on the chamber floor. The women along the wall, dazed, exhausted, and now suddenly overcome with relief, all began to sob at once, releasing emotions that had been building for all the long, horrible days of their captivity. Everett Blaine and Sergeant Drake reached the bottom of the steps just in time to see that it was all over.

Three days later, the entire party of survivors: thirteen British soldiers led by Sergeant Drake, six natives, eight very tired young women, one young American man, and Allan Quatermain, returned to the Natal colony, all looking forward to real beds, better food, and no more danger.

The journey back had been uneventful. The group had camped near the temple that first night, all too tired to travel far. The women had all survived relatively unharmed; their minor wounds were soon cleaned and bandaged. They covered themselves in the blankets brought by the soldiers, which would have to make do until they got new, proper clothes. Sergeant Drake had his men cut down large branches which were roped together to make litters to carry the exhausted women as the trek began. It was slow going at first, but as the trip progressed and the women began to feel stronger, they began to insist on walking. Quatermain made this possible by going off into the jungle and efficiently shooting a number of small furry creatures whose hide was quickly and expertly cut, cleaned, and sewn into primitive shoes for the women. The path seemed shorter then and morale improved. The women even began to sing as they went along, the natives joining in, and soon the soldiers as well.

One week after arriving back at the colony, Everett Blaine stood at the docks, ready to board the vessel that would carry him back to London. He had said goodbye to Katherine already. Most of the women would go back to London, but not her. She had told Blaine that she felt strengthened by her experience and wanted to put that new energy to good use. She would remain at the colony and continue the work she had come to Africa to accomplish, but she would be content to do it in solid buildings that had only just recently been built, and would not venture into the jungle again.

Allan Quatermain had come to the docks with Blaine. Now the two men shook hands. Quatermain's grip was strong and rough; it was the sort of handshake a man only gets by earning it.

"Good luck to you, Blaine. It's been a pleasure to fight alongside you...as much as fighting can ever be considered a pleasure, which it should not."

"Likewise," said Blaine. "Goodbye, sir."

And he boarded the ship, never to set foot in Africa again.

Atlanta, Georgia 1940

"Now I understand why I shouldn't tell Mama you told me that story, Granddaddy."

Everett Blaine laughed. "I haven't told that tale in years, Jeremy, but I can still remember every minute of it."

"And it's all true?"

"I'll leave that up to you to judge, my boy, but tell me, did you get the point of why I told it?"

"To tell me how you became a man?"

"Well that's part of it, Jeremy, and yes, the things that happened to me in Africa made me stronger, tougher, made me grow up real damn fast... but I also meant the example of what I consider to be a real man, the sort of man we should all try to be."

"You mean Allan Quatermain?"

"I do. You see, Quatermain was no intentional hero. He never set out to be a legend or anything. He was an honest man trying to make a living the best way he could, by shooting a rifle maybe better than any man ever did before or since. But when trouble ran up to spit in his face, which it seemed to do often, Quatermain knew how to spit right back at it! Now he didn't like to fight, didn't enjoy killing, but he always did what he had to do, no matter how dangerous it might have been. When a man can do what really, truly needs to be done, that's when he's a man. If you always remember that, Jeremy, you'll grow up just fine."

"Whatever happened to Allan Quatermain, Granddaddy?"

"Well, the funny thing is, Jeremy, that old son of a bitch became quite famous a few years later. Seems he had some experiences after my little adventure with him and he found some fortune, wrote a book about what had happened, and went to London for a time. But men like Quatermain often just can't bear to grow old in places that are too civilized and so he went back to Africa and eventually got himself killed in battle. But you know, Jeremy, I can't imagine what he would have been like as an elderly man, so maybe Fate knew exactly what she was doing sending him out to fight that one last fight."

"And what," Jeremy asked, "happened when you got back to London? Was Major Holloway mad that you didn't bring him a lion's head?"

"Well," Blaine said, smiling, "when I got back to London, I got myself a new suit, got all cleaned up, and went to see the major. He took one look at me, stood up, came out from behind his desk, looked me straight in the eyes, saw that I didn't flinch or look away and said, 'Son, I don't know what you did in Africa, and I don't need to know. I can see that it's changed you…made a solid man out of you. If you still want my Gloria and if she'll have you…then I'm happy to give her to you.'"

"And you married her? But Grandma's name was Helen!"

"Gloria and I had ten wonderful years together, Jeremy. Your grandmother was my second wife, and I loved them both with all my heart. Some may think it's sad that Gloria died young, and believe me, I cried like a baby when I lost her, but it's rare that a man is lucky enough to fall in love twice in one lifetime, so I'll just count my blessings."

Everett Blaine lived to be ninety-one years old. One of his last experiences was saying goodbye to his grandson Jeremy as the young man left home in his brand new uniform to ship off to Korea. Blaine knew that Jeremy would come home not as a boy, but as a man. He hoped he would be the kind of man Allan Quatermain was, the kind who would be capable of doing what needed to be done no matter what.

## THE END

# WRITTEN IN MY SLEEP

It started with a dream. It was as simple as that. I woke up one morning feeling that I should write an Allan Quatermain story. Such a dream surprised me since I really didn't know very much about Quatermain. Sure, I knew he was a well-known character, that his adventures took place in Africa, and that he had inspired such writers, filmmakers, and artists as Edgar Rice Burroughs, George Lucas and Steven Spielberg, and Carl Barks. I knew he had first appeared in H. Rider Haggard's novel *King Solomon's Mines* and that he had appeared in films starring Richard Chamberlain, among others, but my knowledge of Quatermain was nowhere nearly as extensive as what I knew about the other very famous character I've had the privilege to write about, Sherlock Holmes. At that point, I had never even read *King Solomon's Mines*. My only real exposure to Quatermain had been through Alan Moore and Kevin O'Neill's comic book series *The League of Extraordinary Gentlemen* and the film of that name that featured Sean Connery as Allan Quatermain.

I suspect that the dream may have been triggered by the fact that my wife and I were planning to watch *Indiana Jones and the Last Crusade* because she had not seen it and it's one of my favorite films. Indiana Jones was very inspired by Quatermain and so that may have subconsciously suggested to me that I should try my hand at writing Quatermain. Also, I had spent the last few months working on several stories set in modern times and part of my mind may have been itching to get back to writing pulp material set in decades past. Whatever the reasons in the back of my mind might have been, I woke up that morning determined to give Quatermain a shot!

I immediately began to do some internet research on the character and quickly discovered that Allan Quatermain is not exactly what most people who only know him from the movies think (in fact, Connery's portrayal in the League movie comes closer than most other film adaptations despite that being the version that might seem odd to someone who only knows Quatermain from the Richard Chamberlain or Patrick Swayze movies).

Quatermain, as portrayed in *King Solomon's Mines,* is fifty-five years old, hardly a young man. He's also not a tall, handsome movie star-type, but a small, wiry, scruffy man, weathered and hardened by years of life in dangerous places. Upon discovering that Quatermain is not what is shown in most movies, I found him even more interesting. On top of that,

I learned that H. Rider Haggard wrote a lot more Quatermain material than just the one very famous book. Everybody's heard of *King Solomon's Mines,* but what about the other 17 Quatermain stories written between 1885 and 1927?

So I had decided to try to do a Quatermain story. The first thing I did was run out to get a copy of *King Solomon's Mines.* That book was easy to find; it's still in print. The others are harder to hunt down. I read it and made sure I really wanted to work with the character and, having made up my mind, contacted Airship 27's editor, Ron Fortier to ask if he wanted to add Quatermain to our stable of pulp characters. Once I had permission to begin, I threw myself headfirst into the task. I decided against having Quatermain tell the story as Haggard had because I didn't feel I could adjust my style to come close to Haggard's. When I wrote Sherlock Holmes, working within Arthur Conan Doyle's style came somewhat naturally to me since I was so familiar with the Holmes canon, but Quatermain was too new to me and I felt it wiser to do it my own way while still trying to be as true as possible to the character as Haggard had created him. I hope it worked!

Framing the story with the American character, Everett Blaine's telling of the tale to his grandson was something I decided to do to accentuate the idea that Africa, especially over a hundred years ago, might have seemed like a strange place to someone used to living in Europe or America. I wanted a character that was experiencing Africa for the first time in order to have some contrast with Quatermain, who had spent most of his life on that continent and knew its ways very, very well.

Once I began the story, the pieces seemed to fall together and I'm very glad I decided to do it. I hope those of you holding this book in your hands right now will have as much fun reading the story as I had writing it.

Assuming this story goes over well with fans of Allan Quatermain, I suspect this won't be the last time I'll write about that courageous old hunter.

**AARON SMITH** - is the author of 28 published stories, many of them for Airship 27 Productions. His pulp work includes stories in both volumes of Black Bat Mystery, four Sherlock Holmes stories, the Dr. Watson novel *Season of Madness*, and stories featuring Ki-Gor, Dan Fowler, and his own creations, Hound-Dog Harker and the Red Veil. His latest novel is *100,000 Midnights* from Musa Publishing. Information about his work can be found on his blog at www.godsandgalaxies.blogspot.com

# THE VULNERABLE HERO
## BY RON FORTIER

Like most of readers of adventure fiction, I first became aware of H. Rider Haggard's African based hero, Allan Quatermain via the movie adaption of his novel, *King Solomon's Mines* starring the British actor Steward Granger. This is not the first nor would it be the last film version of this classic tale; it remains the most recognized. Other actors who played Quatermain in the movies included Richard Chamberlain, Patrick Swaze, Sean Connery and many more.

So what was it about both this story and this particular character that have so enamored him to readers of adventure fiction? I'd like to suggest it is his vulnerability and the fact that during the course of his life his philosophy changes with the events that shape his life. Rather heady stuff for this kind of pulp figure.

Through Haggard's many stories we learn that Quatermain is an English-born big game hunter and occasional trader in southern Africa. In the beginning he supports colonial efforts to spread civilization in the Dark Continent, though he also favors native Africans having a say in their own affairs. An outdoorsman, he finds English cities and climate unbearable and prefers to spend most of his life in Africa, where he grew up under the care of his widowed father, a Christian missionary.

The natives often refer to him as *Macumazhn*, "Watcher-by-Night," a reference to his nocturnal habits and keen instincts. He is frequently aided by his native servant, the Hottentot Hans, a wise and caring family retainer from his youth. In his final tales, Quatermain was joined by two British companions, Sir Henry Curtis and Captain John Good from the Royal Navy, and his dear African friend, Umslopogaas.

Haggard's Quatermain tales and books cover fifty years of his life, from 18 to 68; at the beginning of the novel, *King Solomon's Mines,* he has just turned 55. He is a small and wiry fellow, referred to as unattractive with a gray-silver beard and short unruly hair. His skill is his uncanny marksmanship. As a professional hunter, he comes to realize that he has helped to destroy the wild free places of Africa that he loved so dearly. As an old man, he continues to hunt as he has no other means of supporting himself.

During the course of the series he lived in both Durban, and in Natal, South Africa and was married twice and tragically widowed both times.

He did have a son named Harry whose death he grieves in the opening of the book, *Allan Quatermain*. Harry was a medical student who died of smallpox while working in a hospital.

As Haggard did not write the Quatermain stories in chronological order, he made mistakes concerning some details. Quatermain's birth, age at the time of his marriages, and age at the time of his death cannot be reconciled with the date of Harry's birth and age at death.

Although some of Haggard's Quatermain novels stand alone, there are two important series. In the Zulu trilogy, *Marie* (1912), *Child of Storm* (1913) and *Finished* (1917), Quatermain becomes ensnared in the vengeance of *Zikali*, the dwarf shaman known as "The-thing-that-should-never-have-been-born" and "Opener-of-Roads." Zikali plots and finally achieves the overthrow of the Zulu House of Senzangakona, founded by Shaka and ending under Cetewayo. These novels are prequels to the foundation pair, *King Solomon's Mines* and *Allan Quatermain* which describe Quatermain's discovery of vast wealth, his discontent with a life of ease, and his fatal return to Africa following the death of his son Harry.

With *She and Allan,* Haggard engineered a crossover between his two most popular franchises, uniting Quatermain with Ayesha, the central character of his hugely successful "She" novels, and bringing in several other key characters from each series—Hans, Umslopogaas and Zikali from the Quatermain series, and Bilali, Ayesha's faithful minister. This book formed the third part of the "She" trilogy, although in chronological terms, it necessarily served as a prequel to the first two "She" books, since Holly and Leo, the protagonists of the first two books, both die at the end of the second novel.

After having published six years worth of stalwart, dashing pulp heroes that were larger than life, the thought of doing a book with Quatermain struck me as a breath of fresh air. I really wanted to see what our writers would do with a character who was as fallible as the rest of us, who had regrets for past sins and yet still managed to keep moving forward; doing his best to do the right thing. Maybe in the end that is the true definition of heroism. Alan Porter and Aaron Smith wonderfully accepted that challenge and their stories are both thrilling and suspenseful, capturing the age of wonder in which this marvelous character was first created.

Another tip of our kepi goes to artists Ingrid Hardy for yet another gorgeous cover and to Clayton Hinkle whose interior illustrations perfectly captured the essence of these wild African adventures, bringing Quatermain and his cast of characters to life visually.

Thanks for joining us on this particular literary safari and we pray you'll return for future volumes. We look forward to your thoughts and comments, both pro and con. After all, we do these books for you, our loyal readers. Thanks always.

*Ron Fortier*
3/10/2013
Fort Collins, CO.
Airship27@comcast.net
(www.Airship27.com)
(http://www.airship27hangar.com)

# SET SAIL FOR ADVENTURE

The greatest seafaring adventurer of all times returns to the high seas, Sinbad the Sailor!

Born of countless legends and myths, this fearless rogue sets sail across the seven seas aboard his ship, the Blue Nymph, accompanied by an international crew of colorful, larger-than-life characters. Chief among these are the irascible Omar, a veteran seamen and trusted first mate, the blond Viking giant, Ralf Gunarson, the sophisticated archer from Gaul, Henri Delacrois and the mysterious, lovely and deadly female samurai, Tishimi Osara. All of them banded together to follow their famous captain on perilous new voyages across the world's oceans.

Writers Nancy Hansen, I.A. Watson and Derrick Ferguson offer up three classic Sinbad tales to rival those of legend while adding a familiar sensibility from the cult favorite Sinbad movies of FX master, Ray Harryhausen. SINBAD – The New Voyages will enthrall and entertain all lovers of fantasy adventure in a brand new way; featuring cover art by Bryan Fowler and twelve black and white illustrations by Ralf van der Hoeven. So pack up your you traveling bags, bid ado to your loved ones and get ready to sail with the tide as Sinbad El Ari takes the tiller and the Blue Nymph sets sails once more; its destination worlds of wonder, mystery and high adventure.

# VOLUME TWO COMING SOON!

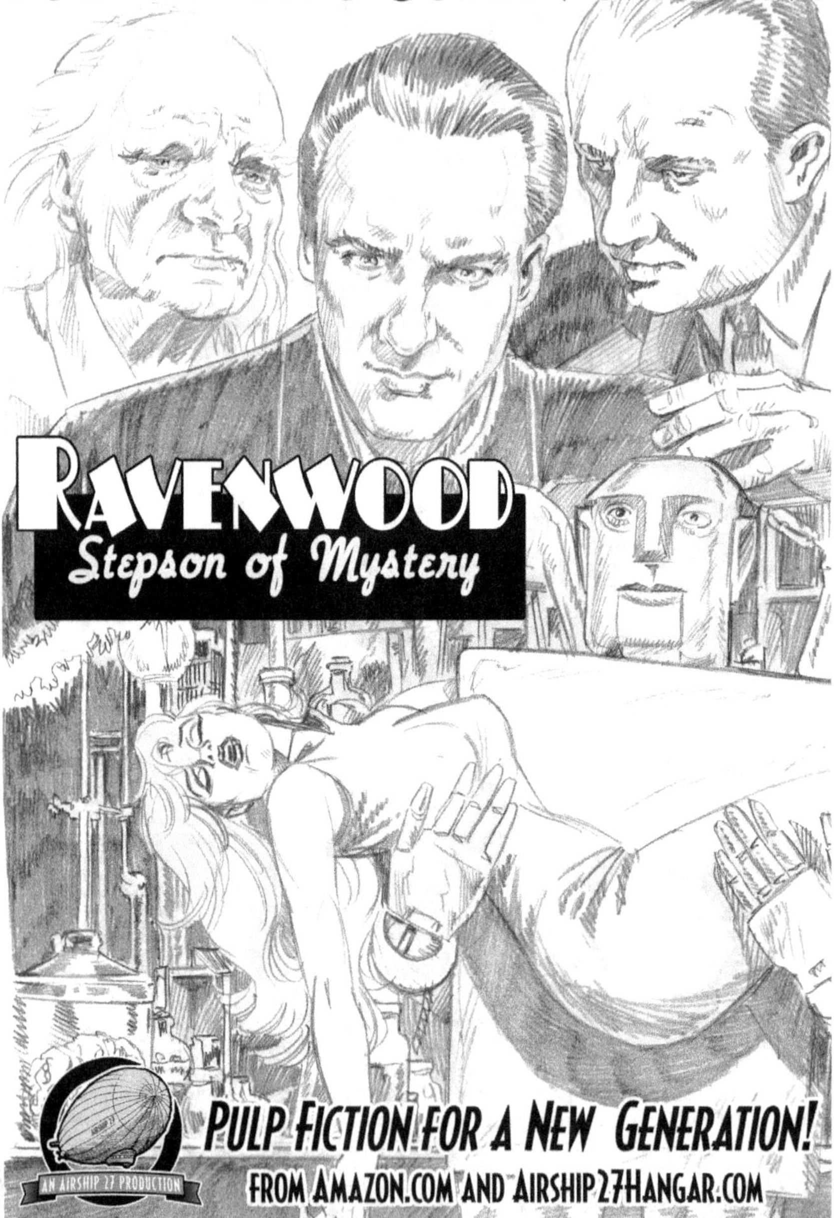